I0665759

'Till Death Do Us Part

'Till Death Do Us Part

Robert J. Moore

MooreWriting Publications

www.MooreWriting.com

'Till Death Do Us Part

Photography provided by:

Cindy Hilditch of Wellington, Ohio

MooreWriting Books may be ordered through your local bookstores or at

www.MooreWriting.com

ISBN: 987-0-6151-8417-3

MooreWriting Publications

This Novel is dedicated to one of my greatest friends, Beth. See you on the other side my friend…

Chapter 1

White was the only thing Nadia saw around her. She couldn't feel anything in her extremities. She wasn't afraid, just calm. Slowly, an image began to focus in front of her. At first, it appeared to be a blemish on a pure white page. As the image became clearer, she could distinguish what it was. It was her sleeping in bed peacefully. She was looking down upon herself. The next thing she heard was a smooth, easy voice lightly radiating through the air.

"Nadia. Naaaadia. Its time to go."

One of the most visually pleasing pictures filled her field of vision. It was a man. He was absolutely one of the most beautiful creatures her light brown eyes ever took in. His face was defined, and chiseled.

He had long shoulder length blonde hair. It wasn't groomed at all. It seemed as if the top of his head had erupted like a volcano and curly yellow flames had dispersed from the top of his cranium and flowed down to his shoulders. He had thin perfect lips. The most striking feature was the radiant green eyes that peered into hers. Those perfect lips inched over the right side exposing a single dimple on his untanned face. She could suddenly feel a sensation in her own lips. She worked up enough energy to mutter out just over a whisper.

"Hey, Honey. Ummm why did you paint a picture of me sleeping over the bed?"

"So you could wake up to the same breathtaking sight that I see every time I wake up next to you."

He thought she was the most beautiful woman in the world. She thought those pretty green eyes of his didn't work. She thought she was far from beautiful. She didn't fit the model type of woman. She wasn't severely obese, but she did carry a voluptuous figure. She did love her vibrant reddish auburn hair. Everyone did. She always kept it quite long and straight. It complimented her eyes so well. She thought she was pretty, but not gorgeous. Whenever she tried to get back down to the size she was before she met her husband, he would always ask her not to. He found her full figure to be quite the turn on. She most likely wouldn't have been too concerned about her size if her friends weren't so extremely thin. He always made her feel good. While lying next to him, he would caress her entire body, not just the most attractive portions. She felt that he loved every part of her, physically and mentally.

"Honey, I love you with all my heart, but if you don't remove that picture of me off the ceiling you;re not going to be waking up to that in the mornings because I won't be sleeping on the couch with you."

"That's why I painted a copy out in the living room."

She instantly could feel the rest of her extremities come alive with his statement and she immediately grabbed one of the pillows off of the bed and fired it in his direction. She was now wide awake.

Today, they were taking a trip to San Diego to attend a conference concerning religion in modern society. Conferences normally separated them during the summer months. She was constantly attending religious conferences while he attended those that dealt with human rights. This was a conference that suited both of them since this conference would conjoin the two topics.

She was a professor of religious studies at The Elyria State University. Her classes weren't the typical religious studies one would normally expect. She dealt with all forms of beliefs. The University was encouraging about her courses because it attracted students from all over the world. Her program was controversial and that controversy brought in money to the school. She also found the topics to be exhilarating. She got to discuss topics on religion that as a child, she would have been grounded for. She was a Christian at heart, but her mind was open. She always felt that there was some sort of connection that all of the religions had. The principles were all the same. Nadia felt that in the end man would get the pieces to the puzzle that was void between people's beliefs. Her parents were not entirely happy with her topics and the attention her program at the University garnered, but they took the same stance as the University and thought of the money it was bringing in. They would make subtle hints to her about her morality, but the glimmer of the designer watches she bought them for Christmas prevented them from hinting too much. Her biggest critic was the ghost of herself. In previous years, she was on her way to being an accomplished scientist until an unforeseen obstacle prevented her from completing her degree in the scientific field. During that time, she doubled as a Sunday school teacher for the local church. Her scientific self sometimes questioned the racy topics she discussed in her classes. Her religious persecuted her for letting herself entertain thoughts that stray from what she had known as the word of God. Despite the inner tug of war, her work satisfied her.

"Tyson did you pack yet?" Nadia asked.

"Did you pack yet?" Tyson responded with guilt.

"Honey, do you think I would be asking you if you packed while I haven't packed yet? Like I'm going to give you the opportunity to make jokes about me being a hypocrite on the plane?"

"That's why I love you baby. You know me so well"

"So did you pack yet?"

"No, but it was on my mind."

Tyson ran his own foundation that benefited civil issues. He could never sit behind a desk and work a typical nine to five. He was extremely intelligent, but he always thought that doing anything in life in a typical fashion would be a waste of his individuality. His foundation fought for human rights throughout Lorain County. His organization established homeless shelters, parenting seminars for pregnant teens, and established animal sanctuaries in the County. He wasn't an absolute resolution to all of Ohio's problems, but he was a good start. Many of the citizens of Lorain County wanted him to run for public office. He declined on a regular basis not that he would become corrupt, but a corrupt system would prevent him from doing his duty. He was in a situation where he felt he could make the most impact. He wasn't in a planning position, he was in a doing position. His free thinking mind was his gavel, the pavement and the forests were his board room. He would not rest until every human had a place to sleep, until there was no more abortion, and there were no more racial discrimination.

"I'm so happy were going to a conference that is relevant to the both of us. I'm especially appreciative that your university is paying for it."

"I'm happy too. It has been too long since the both of us have had a chance to go away together."

Nadia whirled around to look Tyson in his eyes.

"Did you turn off the stove?"

"Yes dear."

"Neighbors taking out the trash and getting the mail?"

"Yes, honey."

"Did you call the cab to pick us up on time?"

"Yes, sugar dumpling."

"Tyson, are you packed yet?"

"Well, are you packed yet?"

Chapter 2

Nadia despised the security line at Cleveland
Hopkins International Airport. Rather she despised the
people that were in it. More specifically, she despised
the people that managed to be efficient in the mornings
and arrive at the airport just before she did, yet never
ready to quickly check through security. She was
always prepared for this. She never carried change in
her pants, she had her laptop out, and made sure her
cell phone was stationed to be scanned. The people
that were ahead of her always held her back. She
thought of the sweet Danish roll and cold orange juice
she could be indulging in at that very moment if not for
the sluggish people in front of her. As Nadia finally
passed through security she felt just as much sadness

for those that were behind her as the anger she felt toward those ahead of her. She was not the reason why she felt terribly sorry for the people behind her, but another reason that she had no control over despite her efforts. That's when she heard the crash.

"I am so sorry everyone. I seem to have dropped my change."

Nadia felt the pain of those standing behind her husband who unlike her was totally unprepared for security.

"Tyson, why would you need change on an airplane?"

"The vending machines sweetheart."

As much as his inappropriate remarks seemed to come at the worst times, his attempts to escape the moment always seemed to coax the ends of her lips to curl into a covert smile. As much as certain nuances of his personality pissed her off at times, those same nuances sent a warm breeze through the inside of her body. His spontaneity is what made him irresistible. He was so naïve to the world, he used it as his playground. He used that very playground to display his love that he had for her. When they were dating, they would often take road trips to random areas of

Ohio. At a truck stop, Tyson decided to buy Nadia a romantic card. Once he discovered that the rest stop only carried obscene cards, he decided to improvise. As Nadia sat in the car she noticed people hurrying out of the truck stop. She was astonished to see her boyfriend with nothing but a box around his pelvic region. The word LOVE was painted down the entire length of his right leg. On the left leg the word YOU was painted on the exact same way.

"Nadia guess who loves you?"
Nadia had no choice to quickly answer as she laughed hysterically.

"I know you do, but please don't remove that box with the answer."

The couple sat in their seats next to each other directly in the middle of the plane. Tyson always wanted to be seated in the middle to represent where he wanted to be in life. Tyson viewed a plane as a representation of the rat race of mankind. Everyone wanted to ride in the front where first class passengers are seated. First class is exclusive to only the few people that can actually afford to fly in luxury. There is a curtain that does not divide the first class from the rest of the passengers on the plane, but to blind the first class passengers from the realities of an economy class flight. The seats were by far too small, and the food was not as desirable. If one passenger decided to recline his or her seat, that person could hear the intense breathing of the angry passenger directly behind that seat. Despite the fact that economy was listed as one class, it wasn't. Money wasn't the dividing factor but location was. The passengers that sat farthest in the back had to wait the longest for service. If the aircraft were to go down, they were the farthest from the exits. The only benefit that people seated in the rear had was the easiest access to the restroom facilities. That was more of a burden because of the grotesque smell that emitted from the room and the constant migration of people that would end up congregating in their small section of the aircraft. The true middle of the airplane represented the true middle class of society. They were a group of people that longed to sit in first class, but wanted no part of the back of the plane unless it was to use the facilities. Nadia always enjoyed the middle for one sole purpose. They would be the closest to the emergency exits just in case if something went wrong.

The movie that was shown on the flight was one of Nadia and Tyson's most cherished movies. It was rather boorish on the plane because all of the good parts were edited out. The flight attendant gradually made her way down the isle of the plane with her metallic gray cart. The usual red apple, turkey club sandwich and graham cracker would be served today. Since the couple had not eaten breakfast they were famished.

They were not accustomed to going without breakfast. That was the time of day when they were able to coordinate their days and schedules. Tyson always liked to know of Nadia's whereabouts just in case he got an uncontrollable urge to be spontaneously romantic. Communicating in the mornings also kept each other in their worlds. They always were interested in every aspect of each other's lives. Tyson's days out in a forest or at a shelter kept Nadia's creativity. Nadia's life in academia kept Tyson grounded. This was not entirely difficult because they hadn't had any children yet. Tyson would mention having children down the road but Nadia never wanted to have any part of that conversation. Tyson always wondered about that because he felt that Nadia would make a wonderful mother. That was one of the main reasons he married her. He knew with his free spirited personality, someone would have to keep the family grounded. Nadia was just that person.

Nadia made every attempt to take a small nap to no avail. The seats were just far too small. No matter what way she tried to organize her body in her confined space, the feeling of irritation would take her over. As she squirmed in her seat, Tyson couldn't help but notice. As her round hips moved from one side to another, her round thighs were halfway exposed in her skirt. He sat there just looking at her neck rock back and forth slightly being splashed by her dark auburn hair. Her slight moans of uneasiness signaled for his adrenaline to his chest. The strong sensation quickly seeped into his shoulder and maneuvered down his arm to his fingertips. He no longer had control of that extremity. It controlled itself. His strong hand had gripped as much of her thigh as it could grab. He slowly and mightily massaged higher and higher up her thigh.

"What do you think your doing?" Nadia asked in a rough, quiet voice. Tyson leaned his head into her neck so she could hear him and he could give her light kisses.

"I'm not doing anything honey. Not anything yet."

"Are you crazy? There are a couple hundred people on this plane. There are kids around. There are elderly people around. Tyson, someone is going to see what you're doing. I'll never fly with you again."

"Then follow me into the bathroom. Nobody can see in there."

Tyson's massaging did not desist. The ear that he had resting on her collarbone that lightly kissed her neck could hear her breathing increase.

"Let's go Nadia. Your membership into the mile high club waits for you in the bathroom."

Nadia was on the brink of succumbing to her husband's suggestions but her sense of awareness smacked her across the face. She quickly brushed his hand to the side and sat up in her chair.

"How about we just relax. We are almost in San Diego. Let's finish this flight without any major drama on this flight please."

"Fine. I guess I will have to go solo."

"Tyson." Nadia called as he walked off to the restroom.

"Not what you think. I drank your pop as well as mine."

Nadia quickly went to reach for her can only to find it completely drained except for the drip that never escapes the can. She went to scold her husband but he was halfway to the restroom.

She sat there in her chair thinking about her husband. She couldn't help but smile at the fond thoughts that tip toed through her mind. He was so sexy. His body and soul all was innocent and erotic at the same time. Those two ingredients combined to make the man she loved. She adored him. She nurtured him intellectually and practically and in return he fed her body and soul with his innocence and eroticism. He kept her body young and alive. He rejuvenated every centimeter of her body with energizing kisses. His touch stimulated every pore of her skin. His words strengthened her cardiovascular system. All these thoughts excited her at that moment in that small seat. He had such an effect on her. Slowly, a thought of mischief intent developed in her. It was her moment to turn the tables on him. She would be the one providing the spontaneity. She would arise from her seat, slowly walk over to the bathroom and sinfully have her way with her husband.

She looked around to see if anyone was paying attention to her. Everyone seemed to be preoccupied with their own agendas. Most of the kids and elderly passengers were asleep. A few others were reading magazines. She stood up. Nervousness almost forced her back in her seat but the slight turbulence forced her motion toward the restroom. She continued her momentum toward the back of the aircraft. She went to knock on the door but the rough skies continued to provoke her wild side. The turbulence had forced her into the door which swung wide open. She caught a glimpse of her husband's face through the mirror in front of the small sink. His eyes had grown twice the size of their normal circumference. His lower lip hung low enough to kiss his own neck. This time it was he who was surprised. This time it was his body and soul who would be consumed by fantasy.

"Well look at this. You decided to step into my world without me pulling you. Let me ask you this. How did you know I wasn't sitting down? What if you came in here and found yourself in a shitty situation?"

Nadia began to feel empowered. It was now her time to be in control of the moment. It was now her time to be the dominate one.

"Good point Tyson. I guess if that were the case I wouldn't have the chance to fuck you in your ass now would I?"

She slowly walked up to him. There they were two flames of passion dangerously lit in a very small, public space. The door to the bathroom was unlocked. Neither made a move to lock it. Nadia forcefully pulled Tyson closely to her. With her right hand, she grabbed his golden hair and forced his head down to hers and gave him an aggressive kiss. Her left hand skillfully unbuckled his belt. His jeans quickly dropped to the floor. She could feel his hands quickly moving all over her back and buttocks. Their breaths quickened and they muscles tightened. Tyson began to flick his tongue across her neck. She ran her hands across the front of his boxer briefs to feel his readiness. He was more than ready. His long and muscular arms quickly swept her up. Her legs swallowed his waste as he gave her chest eager kisses. He slipped her panties out from under her and then turned around and sat her down on top of the sink. She could immediately feel the vibration of the engine pulsating throughout the entire bathroom area. He ripped her sports coat off her body. At that point of emotion and desire, she did not care. Her large breast seemed to fall out of her bra and blouse in one motion. As Tyson's mouth paid close attention to each one she ran her fingers through his hair. At the same time he turned on the water to the faucet. He began splashing the cool water slightly above her knees. He continued wildly splashing the water over her legs. She could feel the trickling water slowly swerve through the light hairs on her legs. With every drop of water, her breath increased. Once she felt the cool water splash on her hot middle, she could feel her insides steam up. Her eyes rolled in the back of her head in pure delight and her legs locked him in inviting him closer. She could feel that he was indeed still ready. His readiness slowly inched up her leg. She couldn't take the anticipation. She felt as if she could not pull him closer fast enough, yet he insisted on taking his time.

The vibrating suddenly turned to shaking in the bathroom.

"Hey maybe we're landing? We better get back to our seats." Tyson said.

"No don't stop. I need you. I need you right here." Nadia insisted.

She tried to pull him closer. At that moment the plane began to shake violently. The contents that were on the single shelf of the bathroom went flying out. One giant shake of the aircraft sent Nadia flying off of the sink and onto Tyson. Out in the plane they could hear screams coming from the other passengers. Instructions were being given out but they could not hear them in the bathroom. Nadia began thinking about their safe seats in the middle of the plane that was right next to the exits.

She regretted giving into her inhibitions. If she would have gone with her sane thinking, they would have been prepared for whatever was happening. But then she wouldn't be with her husband. She would be alone. She immediately grabbed onto him.

"Nadia we have to move. We have to get near the exits!"

They then heard a giant explosion and the plane began to plummet directly toward the earth. Tyson then hit his head on the sink. Blood sprayed all over the bathroom and all over Nadia. She went to lean toward him when suddenly the plane splashed into a body of water. Nadia was then submerged. She could not tell which way was up, down, left nor right. All she could tell was that she was no longer encased in the aircraft. Water was swirling all around her. All she could see was murky red water all around her. Debris quickly flew by her. Bags, metal parts and human parts rushed near her head. She tried to get out of the red stained water. She felt something push on her shoulder and past her. She thought she had been cut on her left shoulder. She had been injured much worse than that. Her arm had been severed from her body. She realized she was going to die if she did not get away from the aquatic chaos swirling all around her. Small artifacts whipped around her slicing her flesh on her arms and face. She could see a light. It must have been the surface. With the little strength and the three extremities she had left, she swam with all of her might to get to the surface. The light seemed to increase the closer the more she swam. Just as she came onto the light with all of her might she leaped up until she had reached her destination.

Chapter 3

Nadia could not hear, see nor feel anything.
All that she knew of was her own existence. She was
not frightened at all. On the contrary, she felt
incredibly at peace. She also knew of her memories.
She let those last fragments of consciousness be her
vision. Her last memories came to her in slight
segments like a recording that had been damaged. Her
memory served as her black box. She remembered
staring into Tyson's intense, willing eyes. Then she
remembered hard water brushing hard against her face.
She could see the things, the people violently dancing
in the maroon water. She could also painfully see the
last vision of her love. His permanently frozen face
was staring back at hers. His giant, glossy eyes were

open looking at her. They did not have the same intensity in them. They lacked the fire and the innocence that she loved. He was gone. His body was just a lovely exterior and no matter how exquisite it appeared, it was void of the true gift that it held. If she had eyes she would cry. If she had limbs, she would shake. If she had a mouth she would yell. All she had was her own consciousness. She knew nothing of life or death. She was just alone with her thoughts. She thought perhaps she was in Hell. She wondered if it could be possible that you are alone with your own thoughts in hell. Before she could complete contemplating this subject any further, she lost the one thing she did have, her consciousness.

The next time she came to, she knew she was still alive. She could feel cool air quickly congregate and disperse in her lungs. With the few muscles she could feel, she inhaled as much of the air as she could and slowly exhaled it. For Nadia, it felt good to be alive. The next thoughts were thoughts that were troubling, yet thoughts she was glad to worry about.

"Where am I?"

"What condition am I in?"

"What happened to everyone else?"

Nadia could feel her consciousness betraying her once more. This time, before she faded, she would fill her lungs with one last gasp of air.

The next time she came about she could feel her eyes. She would attempt to open them slowly. She was fearful what they may capture. She forced herself to peek through her eyelids and was immediately caught by blinding white light. She immediately closed them. She still had no idea where she was, but she knew that her senses and extremities were coming back. It was only a matter of time before she would be fully functional and she could solve the riddles that plagued her mind. She tried to move her arms and legs. She felt sharp pain go through every limb she attempted to move. It was painful, but it was beautiful pain. She relaxed everything and prepared to lose herself once more. This time she would get lost in sleep instead of simply being lost.

When she woke up, she found that she could fully open her eyes. Her vision was blurry, yet she could vaguely make out what things were. The bright white light that had blinded her previously was a florescent light directly over her. The ceiling was a tiled ceiling that was also white. She slightly tilted her head to the left and saw a cylinder machine the height of her bed next to her. A navy blue tube that was roughly four inches in diameter connected her side to this machine. Her vision was far too poor to read the digital readout that constantly changed on the device. She looked to her right and she saw a similar device with similar tubes going into her arms and legs. These tubes were about 2 inches in diameter but many more of them. She could also make out long curtains blowing from a breeze in the window. That explained the addicting air she was breathing in. She could make out an old style stand next to her bed with beautiful white lilies in a vase. She peaked down and looked at the foot of her bed. It seemed as if the design of the bed was also an antique, maybe dating back to the 1950's. After taking all of this in she had a basic idea of where she was, and the next sequence of events confirmed her intuition. She immediately heard the door open and loud talking immediately filled the room. She focused all of her energy to her eyes. She could make out a tall man donned in a long white coat and a clipboard. He was accompanied by two blonde women that appeared to be twins also sporting long white coats. It was only the man who spoke.

"Her condition is much improved. She will be ready shortly. We will notify the office that we have another one. By the time they send someone out, she will be up."

On those words, she fell back to sleep but more peacefully.

"Hello Mrs. McKline. You can wake up now. You will find things quite pleasant this time." A gentle voice said.

She could not help but oblige. It was as if she sat up involuntarily. Precisely in the center of her sight was a man. He was of average height with a very frail build. He appeared to be in his mid 40's. He was bald on the top of his head with remnant of hair on the sides and back of his scalp. He looked back at her with his hazel eyes that seemed to be intensified through his thin glasses. He wore a quaint smile that was intended for her. He wore a beige colored sports coat and eggshell white slacks. His shirt was an exact match to his slacks, while his loafers were an exact match for his sports coat. He wore no tie. Instead, his top two buttons on his shirt were left undone. He was a very sharply dressed man, yet he still appeared to be slightly awkward.

"I'm glad to see you have fully recovered Mrs. McKline. Hello, my name is Peter. You were in and out for a while, but there was never any doubt that you would be perfectly fine."

Nadia then flashed back to the chaos in the water. She was positive that she had lost her arm, yet both of her arms were fully intact.

"Where am I?"

"The best medical facility you have ever been in. It is also the only one we have."

"What happened?"

"Oh that is a very easy question to answer. Perhaps the easiest question you will have. You were bound for San Diego from a flight leaving Cleveland, Ohio when your craft failed and you crashed."

"How are the others?"

"I've talked with the other passengers and they are already processed and taking care of what they need to do as far as their own personal business."

Nadia immediately had a flash back to Tyson looking lifeless at her as he slowly proceeded to drop into the darkness of that water. She was terrified to ask, but she knew she had no choice.

"Tyson, my husband. Did he die?"

At first Nadia refused to allow the truth to enter her mind. She knew he was dead when she saw him there in the water, but it was just an image to her. It did not represent reality. Her mind tried to turn away Peter's truths. No matter how unwelcome those words were they delivered the truth. Such a delivery cannot be turned away from the soul.

Once the fact that Tyson had died in the plane crash began to set in, Nadia slowly began a decent into insanity. She felt her arms and legs begin to shake. Her eyes began to concentrate to the point where they felt as if they were going to explode out of her head. Lightening strikes began tormenting her head. It felt as if her body was beginning to self destruct. Her body was a bomb that was triggered by an extreme loss. A loss so great that she would refuse to exist without her love. Her dry, chapped lips began to contort themselves into unrecognizable positions. Large tears began to run out of her eyes that looked like red volcanoes ready to erupt. She couldn't help but continuing to murmur his name repeatedly. All of her erratic conditions began to intensify to the dismay of Peter. He felt so uncomfortable, that his own body began to tremble.

"Mrs. McKline, what is the matter?"

Her arms and legs began to flail around and her body began to gyrate uncontrollably. The path to insanity was well underway.

"My husband is dead! He's gone! My poor, poor Tyson. I love you Tyson. I love you Tyson! He's gone!"

"Ummm Mrs. McKline."

"He's gone!"

"Mrs. McKline."

"He's gone!" Nadia continued to yell.

"Mrs. McKline."

"I won't be able to see him anymore!"

"Well that's not true Mrs. McKline."

"What in Hell do you mean it's not true?"

"Once we get you ready, you can begin your search for him."

"How am I supposed to look for my husband that you just told me is dead?"

"Now we have reached the toughest question with the toughest answer. You can begin to look for your husband because you also are dead Mrs. McKline. By your definition of course."

Nadia could not believe the words that escaped Peter's breath and radiated to her ears. She sat up on the bed never removing her sight off Peter. Her mouth remained fixed in an open position. If all of the shocking revelations of the day had numbed her, this last one awakened her. She didn't feel dead. It felt like any other day. She could smell the breeze. The sun's arms touched down and caressed her face. These things were signs of being alive, not dead. What would she do now? Where would she go? Where did she go? All these questions lingered in her head. Then she realized what Peter had said.

"Once we get you ready, you can begin your search for him."

With the hope of reuniting with Tyson, she knew she had to pull herself together. She fixed her hair with her hands and wiped away the snot from her nose and the tears away from her red eyes.

"What's the next step? What do I have to do to find Tyson?"

"All in due time Mrs. McKline. First I must give you a tour, some rules and regulations, and most importantly a place to stay. In the next room there is a shower and some clothes for you. The sooner you are ready, the sooner we can be on our way.

Nadia showered and dressed herself as quickly as possible. She was eager to find out the answers to her questions. The clothes were something she would typically wear when going to work. She was dressed in a navy blue knee length skirt, with a matching Sports coat. Her blouse was a white button down shirt that was accented with white stripes. As she stepped from the room she could see how embarrassed Peter was. She could immediately tell he was shy around women. To make him feel more comfortable, she buttoned one more button not to expose so much of her full cleavage. Peter tried the best he could to hide his awkward embarrassment.

"There are many different forms of transportation here. There is public transit that can take you from place to place, flight, or by personal vehicle. For the sake of time, we will travel by teleportation. Citizens are not permitted to travel by teleportation. Only government officials are allowed to travel that way. I will not even show you nor anyone how it's done. Are you ready Mrs. McKline?"

"I am as ready as I'll ever be."

Nadia was ready to venture out in her new world. She was ready to experience whatever was out there waiting for her. She only wished she had the love of her past life to experience it with. She accepted Peter's open elbow with her own arm and held on tight. She was ready to start her new existence.

Chapter 4

Nadia could not tell the last instant she was in the hospital from the moment she was in her new location. Wherever she was, it was night. She could see stars in the sky twinkling like white Christmas lights. The moon was also a magnificent white. It appeared to be twice the size of the moon that she had known on Earth. If the moon had shoulders; they would have been kept warm by the colorful scarf that was made by the northern lights draped around the sky. Crystal like snowflakes the size of maple leaves fell from the night sky. Unlike average snowflakes, the designs were all clearly visible to the human eye. Nadia was greeted with a friendly tickling sensation from the snowflakes that managed to find her face. It was if the moon was sending a courtesy down to her.

Nadia then realized that she was standing on a small dirt path in a wooded area. She visually surveyed the area. All around her she could see the heads of deer, chipmunks, woodchucks, and field mice looking at her. They didn't seem to be the least bit afraid of her. They just stood there studying her, reflecting her own curiosity. She looked back up the path and saw a collection of bright lights. She began walking down the path towards the lights. As she drew closer to them, it became apparent that those were the lights of a small village. No building could be more than 2 stories high. There were different varieties of buildings. Some appeared to be log cabins and some looked as if they were made of wood and stone. It looked like a winter wonderland.

When she finally made it to the town she could see people shopping and drinking and singing joyful songs. Children pulled each other on sleighs. Dogs were playfully eating snow right off of the ground. She then realized that she wasn't wearing any winter attire at all, yet she was completely comfortable. Her naked legs felt as if she were in a 72 degree room. Her ears and fingers felt equally as comfortable as her legs.

"Comfort is not a problem here. We are dressed totally different, yet we both feel the same."

Nadia looked to her left and there standing was Peter. He had the biggest winter hat on his head that made his head appear four times its normal size. With the combination of his oversized hat and his extra puffy scarf, you could hardly tell it was him if not for his distinct pointed nose and glasses. His red flannel winter coat and brown boots were also too large for his thin frame. Nadia giggled to herself as she imagined that Peter was a clothes hanger supporting the winter gear in a closet.

"Even though you're not cold you must try some of the hot cocoa here. I guarantee that it will be the best you have ever had."

They both entered Milner's, a small café on the main street. There appeared to be only fifty or so candles in the venue, yet the room was lit as if it were filled with thousands. There was a center bar area, along with two long bar areas far to the right and left in the room. There was a section that was designated as a dance area where teenage children practiced various line dances with laughter falling out of their faces. There were a couple of lounge areas equipped with fireplaces and large sized couches where men and women consumed their libations in the midst of pleasant conversation.

Nadia followed Peter over to the far left bar. They sat down at two stools and waited for the bartender to come over. She looked at the endless bottles that were behind the bar. The bottles made up an impressive array of colors. None of them wore a label.

"What is this place, Peter?"

"Not what, but where. Yes, it is what you think but where in what is the key. We are in a suburban area of the place that you are thinking of. The name of where we are is called Tundral. You see, the idea of Utopia is different to different people. This is the ideal place for people that enjoy a winter setting. In time we will visit all of your options."

"Well look who we have here. If it isn't Mr. Peter. He's the only man who is outweighed by the clothes on his back."

Despite Peter's inclusion with the entire bar's laughter, he did not enjoy the bartender's poke at him.

"What is your new girlfriend's name, Peter?"

"This is Nadia. She is not my girlfriend. She is my new case."

"Well hello there Nadia. My name is Mr. Milner. It is my pleasure to have you here in my establishment."

Mr. Milner looked as if he could be Santa Claus' brother. He was an extremely large man in mass and height. He had a wild, burly beard that donned the colors black, gray, and a little reddish brown. The hair on the top of his head was identical to his beard. He wore a white dress shirt with large black pants and matching suspenders.

"Here Sweetheart, try the house special."

Nadia looked inside the large mug to see her reflection in liquid that was dark as oil. She would have turned the mug away if the steam that emitted from the drink did not smell so good. She lifted the mug and nodded in appreciation to Mr. Milner just before she took her first sip with her eyes closed so she could not see the dark drink. Instantly her mouth felt happy. She could feel the slightly warm drink slowly progress down her throat. She took a deep breath as it slowly made its way through her body. It felt as if it was not only going through her digestive system, but through her blood stream. She felt buoyancy in her hands and feet. The tingling sensation made her shudder with delight. She looked at Mr. Milner with wide eyes. Before she could comment on the drink, he already had the answer for her.

"You're Welcome."

She could not help but to laugh she felt so good.

"Here you are Mr. Peter. Your usual drink and it's on the house for bringing such a beautiful woman into my place of business here."

A smile streaked across Peter's face as he raised his glass that contained a dark blue substance. Peter downed the drink in one gulp. Immediately his face turned red as a rose and his eyes doubled in diameter. His neck was strained to the point to where you could see his veins. He quickly reached for the flask of water on the bar and downed it. Everyone at the bar erupted in laughter.

"Mr. Milner, you know that is not my drink. I cannot drink alcohol on the job."

"Awww I'm just having a little fun with you there Mr. Peter. Please don't take it personal. I'm going to liven you up one of these days."

"I appreciate the concern but this is not the time."

There was another question that was bothering Nadia. She dared not ask Mr. Milner about this, but instead turned to Peter.

"How can it be that drinking is allowed here?"

"Thank you Mr. Milner, but I must be going so I can show Nadia her other options. You have a good day Sir."

"You are quite welcome, Mr. Peter. It was a pleasure meeting you, Nadia. Please visit us again."

"Thank you Mr. Milner. It was a pleasure meeting you. It was a pleasure meeting you all. I will make sure to visit you all again."

Peter put on his oversized hat and his oversized scarf. He then walked with Nadia to the door and down the path back to the wooded area. Just as before, he held out his arm waiting for Nadia to intertwine hers. She couldn't remember the last time she had so much fun. What she truly was thinking was the last time she had so much fun without Tyson. Her thoughts then went back to him. She needed to stay focused on finding her husband. She did enjoy her brief stay in Tundral, but there were more pressing matters to attend to. Once she found Tyson, she would bring him back to Tundral for drinks and laughs. The only question was how soon this would happen.

Chapter 5

Just as before, Nadia could not determine the moment she left Tundral from the moment she was in her new setting. The first thing she saw was beautiful palm trees surrounding her. She looked down to see a small crab lightly picking at the toe of her shoe. She could hear the movement of a large body of water. In the case that her ears were deceiving her, her nose would assure her by presenting her with the fresh, open smell of water. She could also hear voices in the distance. As soon as she stepped out from behind the palm trees, she noticed that the sun was setting, yet its shine was brilliant. Just as the moon was in Tundral, the sun seemed to be much larger than the one she was accustomed to. Nadia thought she would have needed to shade her eyes with such a bright sun but she did not. She did not need to wince her eyes and there was no need for shades. She walked through the white sand down to the bluest water she had ever seen. It was so clear she could see the multicolored gravel at the bottom of the water. She stuck her hand in the water to feel the temperature. She could not have guessed that the water would feel so good. The moment she stuck her fingers in, there were various fish of different sizes but none larger than her thumb lightly nibbling at her hand. She was amazed at the various colors they were painted with. She could not resist slipping off her shoes and slipping her feet into the moisturizing water. When she lifted her head she could see there were people down the coastline. She began to walk toward them.

When she reached the others she could see that there were many activities taking place. There were many people in the water swimming, floating, and surfing. All of the females were dressed in cute two piece bathing suits. She then realized that despite her still wearing her business attire, the temperature there also did not make her feel uncomfortable. She was not the least bit hot. All of the gentlemen were wearing either swimming trunks or Speedos. There were couples lying together all over the beach. It made her think of Tyson, but her spirits stayed up. She thought about bringing him here and lying on the beach staring at the brilliant sun together. Tyson loved to surf and this would be his ideal spot.

She spotted a group of kids surrounded by an elaborate sand castle. She ventured over to them.

"This must be the biggest, most beautiful sand castle I have ever seen. You all should be very proud of yourselves. How long did it take you to make it?"

"Thank you for the compliment, Miss. We all worked on it together. Each one of us brought a positive attribute to the project and amazing things took place."

Nadia studied each one of the kids surrounding the immaculate sand castle. They all appeared to be of early elementary school age. The girl that first spoke to her was of Indian decent with a British accent. There was an African boy and two Spanish girls. Despite their youth, there seemed to be something mature about them. The girl seemed well versed and they all had an eerie composure about them. They all seemed to posses pleasant personalities. They had brilliant smiles and were very polite. The only uneasy feature about the children was their eyes. Each one had a set of dark eyes that looked almost black. Their eyes seemed to be more like camera lenses. Their eyes resembled those of a raven's to Nadia.

"I'm not sure how long it took us to create this castle. We were not overly concerned about the time. When we get it finished wasn't a concern as much as will we get it finished."

The castle was amazing with its intricacies. The domed roof and the many windows appeared to be so detail oriented. You could see the variations of textures that were used.

"May I ask your name, Ma'am?" the girl asked.

"Nadia. Her name is Nadia," the African boy said in a low voice. Instantly, the two Spanish girls flashed him a look that could have easily cut through any of the tree in a forest.

"How did you know my name?"

"How silly of him. He forgot you told us your name when you first introduced yourself. Please forgive him for his lack of immediate retention," the Indian girl quickly answered.

Nadia could not remember if she had told them her name or not. She quickly forgot the incident once the girl flashed her smile again.

"It was nice meeting you all. Perhaps I'll see you all again sometime."

"I'm sure you will, Mrs. McKline," the African boy said.

This time Nadia was positive she had not given out her last name or the fact that she was married. Before she could figure out what was going on, her attention was directed behind her.

Nadia felt a light brush on her calf muscle. She turned around to see a white volleyball staring back at her.

"I'm sorry, the ball kind of got away from us."

Nadia looked up to see a gorgeous woman with an ethnic tan staring at her. She had shoulder length, black curly hair with dark brown eyes. She sported a radiant smile that was accented by cute dimples. She appeared to be in her early twenties.

"Hey would you like to join us? The more the merrier."

"Oh no, I'm not really dressed for it."

"Well you are wearing panties and a bra aren't you?"

"Yes, I do but..."

"Well it's settled. Take off your clothes and join us. You better hurry before someone takes your place."

In haste, Nadia immediately began to unbutton her sport coat. Despite her haste she could not get her sport coat off. A powerful force prohibited her from undoing the final button. Nadia realized the superior physical condition most of the people there were in. She would surely get laughed at. At the moment she needed a miracle the most, a miracle was granted to her.

"She doesn't have time to play volleyball. We won't be here very long."

"Well that's just too bad Peter. We could have used you both."

The joy that was brought to Nadia's face could not be hidden. It was so obvious, that Peter immediately began to blush. She wanted to hug him very badly, but she feared that if she did, his frail body would either break in half or he would die of embarrassment. Peter was wearing an oversized T-shirt with long shorts that went down three quarters of his legs. His socks covered his feet which were encased in brown sandals. She could see how Peter was such a klutz. His flattened feet were oversized for his slim stature.

"Peter, why are you wearing floaters on your arms?"

"We are very close to the water. I could easily slip in and drown," Peter said in an agitated voice. That could only make Nadia giggle at his mood. Peter was ready to change the subject.

"This place, Nadia, is called Dundon. As you can see this suburb has a beach setting. There are cottages further in the woods. This is more of a laid back area."

Peter did not realize that his words were being wasted. Nadia's attention was somewhere else. Somewhere he did not know about. A place that he could not show her despite it was in plain view. In Nadia's view was a tall, slender man with golden, shoulder length hair. The muscles on his back looked so familiar. She would hold onto them every night. At that moment, everything went in slow motion except for him. What she thought she would have to search for was directly in front of her.

She took off running across the beach. She ran so hard she could not hear Peter calling for her. The only thing she could hear was the warm air whispering encouragements to her to achieve her goal. Her tears flew back across her cheeks and into her hair. She dared not take time to wipe them. She stumbled over a lunchbox that belonged to a lounging couple, but was immediately backed on her feet running towards him yelling so loud she could not hear her own cries.

"Tyson! Tyson!"

When she finally reached the man she nearly knocked him over into the crowd of people he was talking to.

"Who are you lady?" the man asked as his friends laughed at the scene.

It was not her beloved Tyson as Nadia had hoped.

She slowly sank to her knees as the crowd walked away. Her face began to itch as the tears rolling down her cheeks intertwined with the sand on her face. Her sports coat was open and sand covered her blouse. Her hair was a mess and she was sweating and breathing heavy as her heart exploded and poured out of her eyes. She was convinced it was Tyson. She wanted it to be Tyson. She missed him so much. She could not remember the last time she had such a letdown.

        She looked up to see Peter standing over her with his hand outstretched. Without saying a word, she stood up and tried to compose herself. She tried to straighten her hair with her hands. She wiped the tears and sand solution from her face. She dusted the sand off from the rest of her and buttoned her sports coat. She was still a mess but she was determined to pretend not to be. She looked over her shoulder to see the kids that were making the sandcastle staring at her with black stares. Their dark, intense eyes made her feel cold. She turned back around and saw Peter's arm waiting for her.

Chapter 6

Nadia stood completely still on the concrete sidewalk as hundreds of people scurried past her as if she was blue mailbox. The sidewalks and streets were filled with people dressed in business attire and briefcases as accessories. Men and women were guided by instinct alone as their eyes and ears were focused on their cell phones and mobile devices. Despite the uniform style of dress, there were different men and women of different ethnic backgrounds, genders shapes and sizes. Nadia also noticed that there was a light rain falling, yet no one was neither wet nor carried umbrellas. She looked to the sky to find that skyscrapers that seemed to go up to the atmosphere surrounded her. She did not know which way to go or where to turn to. She looked around for Peter, but he was no where to be found. She just stood there trying to gather her thoughts. Nadia realized that she could not stay in that one spot forever. She attempted to stop someone and ask where she was.

"Get out of my way lady! I have business to conduct," seemed to be the standard answer.

Nadia's hunger pains began to take her mind off of being lost. She was so hungry she could have eaten a skunk and would have been grateful. She thought since she was in a major city setting, a street corner would have a hotdog cart. She placed herself in the current of people that was moving toward the direction she wanted to go. Sure enough, on the next corner, there was a hotdog cart. There was a man that was stationed at the cart. He appeared to be near the age of fifty years. He wore a bright orange wool hat. It was obvious that he had not shaven in two or three days. He wore a red flannel shirt with a blue vest over it. He wore black wool gloves that had the fingers cut out of them.

"What do you want Honey? You gotta be quick or else you're gonna hold up my line."

"What do you have?"

"I got filet mignon on a bun, Sweetheart. What in the hell does it look like I have? I got what every other hotdog stand has ever had in the history of hotdog stands. Now c'mon and pick something damn it!"

Nadia could not fathom how a man so cruel was accepted in paradise. This was the behavior she would expect back on Earth. When she and Tyson would go to Cleveland to catch a Browns' game, the street venders were always kind to her.

"She will have two standards and a cola. I'll take two of my usual."

"Sure thing Peter."

The man handed Peter two regular sized hotdogs equipped with mustard and ketchup along with a regular sized soda. Peter handed them to Nadia. The man then proceeded to hand Peter two large sized hotdogs loaded with mustard, ketchup, relish, jalapeño peppers, coleslaw, and baked beans. He then handed him a large sized soda. The both of them found a bench nearby and sat down to eat. Nadia was so hungry, she quickly devoured her first hotdog.

"Ummm you have ketchup on your blouse there," Peter pointed out.

At first, he grabbed his napkin and was going to help as a gentleman should, but embarrassment overtook him. Nadia attempted to wipe it out herself but it just smeared, leaving a noticeable stain on the top of her blouse. She looked at the mess the sand from Dundon had left. She was a mess.

"Is this the main city, Peter?"

"No. Despite the size of this suburb, it's still a suburb. This place is called Urbanopolis. As you can see, this suburb is designed for those who like the fast paced city life. Most of the business is conducted here. All of the major corporations are stationed in Urbanopolis."

"Hold on. I always thought everyone would be taken care of. How can there be an economy here if there are no people of need or want?"

Without even taking his eyes off of his hotdogs which were quickly vanishing, Peter answered her question.

"No matter when or where you are, humans will always have a want. Needs can be fulfilled, but the want will always exist. To further answer your question, on Earth the economy was uneven. There were entire countries in famine, and yet there were other countries in an abundance of wealth. Here there are different levels of status, but there isn't anyone that is starving or suffering. Everyone is at least well off doing what they love to do. There is a harmonious balance. A balance that can never be broken."

Nadia was amazed at what she had heard. She never thought that a truly perfect economy was possible.

"There are other things here besides business. There are theaters, nightclubs, and parks. In fact, I would like to show you. Are you going to eat your last hotdog?"

Nadia was astonished that Peter had already eaten both of his large hotdogs. She shook her head giving him permission to eat her last hotdog. In two bites, the hotdog no longer existed.

"How can you fit so much food in your rail thin body?"

"Well, I am a very busy man and I never sleep. I guess in order to keep the furnace going you have to keep a large supply of coal in the fire. Let's go I want to show you the entertainment district of the suburb."

The two picked up their trash, disposed of it in the trash bin, and started their walk down the block.

After walking four blocks that seemed to slowly slope downward, they arrived at their destination. Nadia looked around at the few blocks that were full of an array of entertainment spots. People walked through the streets holding large white Styrofoam cups. The rain had stopped, but the streets were still wet so the lights from the buildings were reflected off of the pavement. There were different nightclubs for different things. There were comedy clubs, dance clubs, and bars. There was a riverboat that illuminated the water as it gently glided down the river. Nadia was shocked to see that there were even adult entertainment clubs.

"In Cleveland, we have an area like this called The Flats. I would go there when I was in college to party," Nadia reminisced.

"Well you can do the same thing here."

"Not what I would do down there," Nadia said under her breath.

Nadia and Peter walked into a nightclub called, The Kat's Klub. There was no one at the door to check for proper dress or identification. The air was filled with blaring Hip Hop music. The place was full of people, yet there was just enough room to maneuver.

"Hey how about going to a café? It's much more quiet in there."

Despite Peter's request, Nadia did not acknowledge him because she couldn't hear him. She saw that his face was contorted from the smoke in the air. She did not plan to stay for long. She just wanted to have one drink and listen to one song. Her spirits had been in constant decline since the incident in Dundon. She took a firm grip on Peter's hand and pulled him to an open spot on the dance floor. This time it was Peter who was experiencing rigor mortis. Nadia was no stranger to a dance floor. She began to dance provocatively in close proximity to Peter. Halfway through the song, Peter could not handle the intensity of Nadia's smooth motions.

"Hey uhhhhh let's sit for a moment."

"Ok you party pooper, I'm going to go have a drink and then we can move on."

Nadia proceeded over to the bar. An attractive blonde was manning the bar.

"I would like a cranberry stoli please."
The bartender immediately fixed Nadia's drink.

"That will be four dollars and fifty cents."

Nadia realized that she did not have any money to her name. She was not even sure what form of currency was used.

"Honey, if you don't pay for that drink, you and I will have a big problem."

"I got her covered."

There was a young man that barely looked twenty one. He was wearing a sleeveless sweater that left his tattoos on his arms exposed. He wore a pair of khakis and all white tennis shoes. The sides of his head were shaven with the top slicked back and blonde.

"You must be new around here."

"Yes I am. Thank you for buying me my drink."

The young man slowly moved his stool closer to hers. He constantly kept lightly touching her leg. She was not the least bit flattered at the attention. The only man she wanted to touch her was Tyson. It was obvious to her that he did not buy her drink out of chivalry, but he thought he was purchasing the rights to her time.

"Thanks for the drink, but I must be on my way now."

As Nadia went to get up and walk away, she found that the young man had a grabbed her by the arm.

"Where do you think your going? I haven't even finished my drink yet."

"I thanked you for the drink and now I must go. Now please let go of my arm."

The young man tightened his grip and pulled her close.

"You bitches are all the same. A guy shows you a little attention and you think your too damn good."

Fearing for her safety, Nadia tried to pull away. She yelled but no one came to her rescue. She tried to jerk away so hard, she thought she was going to dislocate her shoulder. In the struggle, the young man bumped into a guy standing behind him.

"Son of a bitch, you made me spill my drink over my white shirt."

"Kiss my ass," The young man yelled back.

Immediately, the offended man picked up a beer bottle off of the bar, and proceeded to smash it over the head of the young man. Everyone in the club began screaming and scattering out of the club. Peter grabbed Nadia's hand and guided her to the exit. As they were going outside, the police were making their way inside, with clubs drawn. Peter and Nadia stood on the sidewalk away from the melee gasping for breath.

"I don't understand this place, Peter. I don't understand things at all. There are so many poor attitudes. People drinking and fighting. Look across the street. There are strip clubs for crying out loud. Why is there even need for police?"

"Things aren't exactly the way they are told in stories," Peter answered as he held out his arm.

Chapter 7

Nadia stood in front of a dirt path that snaked up a long way to a simple looking two-story house. The house was entirely white. It had brick red shutters on the two downstairs windows as well as the single upstairs window. The house was crowned with a chimney. The entire property was surrounded by a white picket fence made of wood. The fence was so small it was apparent that it was strictly for design. The gate was ajar, beckoning Nadia to walk forward.

As she walked forward, a golden retriever ran up to her and began barking while it leaped into the air with its tail wagging. The shining sun brought out the vibrant color in the dog's coat. A five year old girl sitting in the rich, green grass called the dog. As soon as the dog detected its name it went galloping toward the girl and laid next to her. Nadia had reached the porch and proceeded to walk up the stairs. She spotted a large swing. She sat down for a brief moment. She did not swing, but she wanted to catch the scenic view. The girl ran with a bubble blower in her hand as the dog chased after her. She could see the green grass dance back and forth in the warm breeze. The only thing missing was ice cold homemade lemonade in a tall glass. Her moment was up and it was time to see who was home. This time around, Peter was nowhere to be seen. Nadia thought perhaps she would have a chance to wash her clothes and take a shower before he showed up. She would have to hurry, but she thought she may have time. She rang the doorbell expecting a frail old woman to answer the door with that glass of lemonade in hand. She was greeted by a familiar face instead.

"Peter."

"Hi Nadia. Come on in. Everyone is out back."

Nadia walked through the front door into the living room. There was a large sofa with a multicolored cover over the back of it. The sofa itself was a moth color with multicolored flowers in the print. There were two identical wooden rocking chairs placed at opposite ends of the small living room. There was no television, only a large radio with a record player built on the top. The walls were nearly completely covered with family pictures. The next room was a small kitchen. There was an old fashioned stove and fridge. The fridge also carried many pictures on the cover. There was a small round wooden table covered with a white cloth. The door in the back of the kitchen led outside to the back porch. Nadia stepped outside and witnessed with her own eyes how vast their land truly was. The grass went on as far as the eye could see. In the far off right, she could spot rows of corn and other planted produce. To the center of her view she could see a collection of barns which were the origins of the sounds of farm animals. To the far left she could see a private lake with a small row boat docked on the side. Immediately at the bottom of the steps that led down from the back porch was a table. There sat an elderly man and woman. The couple looked to be in their eighties. The man wore a white dress shirt with faded black suspenders and gray slacks. He also wore a straw hat. His wife wore a long red and white dress with ruffles around the thick shoulder straps. When they saw Nadia and Peter, they all flashed an inviting smile. The elderly gentleman took off his straw hat, exposing the few strands of white hair he had left. Nadia returned their smiles with one of her own as she and Peter joined them. She was pleased to see the pitcher of ice cold lemonade she anticipated.

"Nadia, these are friends of mine. This is Frank and Joanne. This is their farm. They have lived here as far as I can remember. Frank, Joanne, this is Nadia."

Nadia noticed that Peter seemed much more comfortable here than any of the previous suburban cities. She could see why. Peter's personality was very reserved, very shy. Most of the other places were fast and social. In a way, the farm reflected Peter.

"It's a pleasure to meet you both."

"The pleasure is all ours, young lady. My gosh. You are so beautiful," Joanne responded. As the woman poured everyone a glass of her delicious lemonade, she continued to find out more about Nadia.

"So what brings you here?"

"Plane crash."

"Oh my. I hope it was quick and painless," Frank added.

"To be honest, I can't remember much about it."

A flash of the watery scene came back to Nadia. She could clearly see Tyson's fixated face staring up at her as his body slowly sank into the depths of the cold water. That was the last images she knew of her husband. With these images playing in her mind, it triggered an emotional reaction. Her nose and eyes matched her auburn hair color. Her breathing increased. She felt as if she was still laying in the hospital bed when Peter first told her about her husband.

"Are you alright dear?"

"She will be fine. She just needs air. Is it alright if I show her around?"

"Sure Peter, be our guest. We have to run to Tundral to pick up a few things. You both should stop by for dinner sometime."

Nadia and Peter took a stroll down the dirt path that led to the barns that contained the farm animals.

"Is this your favorite place?" Nadia asked.

"Here in Rurlaw? No there is one secret place that I hold dear to my heart."

"Will we get a chance to go there?"

"Then it wouldn't be a secret," Peter jokingly replied.

Nadia took time to look at the sheep. They looked like walking clouds.

"Is your secret place where your wife and kids are?"

"Huh?"

"You know, wife and kids. Your family. Where do they stay?"

"I don't have a family," Peter answered in a quiet voice."

"I think you work too much. You should find a good woman, settle down and have some children."

"Some of us just were not meant to have children, or get married. Some people are too busy, some people prefer not to. For some, it just wasn't meant to be. I can't imagine there being anyone out there for me. I have a purpose and a family life isn't one of those."

As Peter explained his situation, his voice began to trail off. Nadia could sense hopelessness in

his voice. A hectic schedule wasn't the reason why
Peter did not start a family. Despair filled his heart.
Nadia took his hand.

"There is someone for everyone," she said with
a smile.

Peter looked up at her. His eyes were glossy
with emotional liquid. The tip of his pointy nose was
red as well as his cheeks. For the first time, Nadia
witnessed him crack a genuine smile.

"Maybe someday I will start a family," Peter
said with hope in his voice as he motioned for Nadia to
take his arm.

Chapter 8

Once again Nadia found herself walking on a
sidewalk in an urban area. This time classic buildings
collected from the annals of time replaced the tall
skyscrapers from Urbanopolis. There seemed to be
tens of thousands of people under the age of twenty
five walking in the streets and around the buildings.
Nadia looked up and saw that she was standing next to
an enormous structure that was identical to The
Coliseum. All of the young people carried backpacks.
Some were sprawled in comfortable positions in the
grass with their faces contorted in concentration trying
to master what was presented to them in their books. It
was obvious to Nadia that she was in the center of a
college campus. She had never seen a campus this

enormous. She studied the circumference of her surroundings and the campus seemed to go on forever. Unlike the other suburbs, she felt as if she knew where she was and where she had to get to. She began walking to where she needed to get to. She took in all of the names of the buildings during her stroll. Most of the buildings were made of stone or brick. They all were very large and tall. There seemed to be a park or a resting place on every block. She came to an intersection that appeared to be the main street.

"High Street," Nadia whispered to herself.

High Street had all of the allures that all typical college campuses had. There were quite a few bars lined down the street. The only thing that separated the bars on the street were sandwich and pizza shops. She could hear the familiar sounds of a live band playing from inside one of the establishments. At that moment, she realized that she missed being at work at Elyria State. She missed her students. She missed being in the classroom. Those memories hit her, literally.

"Hey I'm sorry for running into you, Lady. Hey wait your Professor McKline."

"Rodney?"

"Yes it's me in the flesh. Well not in the flesh of course."

A scrawny kid stood in front of Nadia. His hair was a mess and his sleeveless T-Shirt exposed his thin arms nearly covered in ink.

"Are you going to school here?"

"Yeah, and staying out of trouble. I am retaking your class on religion and I think here its going to be a breeze. All of my other credits transferred."

"Are you telling me that the administration at this University contacted Elyria State and got your transcripts?"

"Here everyone's records are open," Rodney said with a smirk.

"I'm sorry but I have to go, I'm late for work. Good seeing you Mrs. McKline. Well under the circumstances of course."

Nadia could not believe what she was hearing. Rodney was one of her worst students. He hardly showed for her class. When he was there his work was atrocious. He didn't look happy to actually be putting effort toward anything but he was and that's what mattered to Nadia.

Nadia continued on her trek to where she was going. She didn't know exactly where she was headed, but she knew how to get there.

Nadia finally walked a few more blocks until finally arriving at her destination. She arrived at a one story and very average looking red brick building. There appeared to be no windows. There were about twenty steps leading up to the glass doorway that was made of tinted black glass. There were no markings on the building or no signage but this is where she was meant to go. When she entered the building she could tell it was an administrative building. There were elevators to her left and right. The hallway was lined with different offices and organizations. She was meant to go straight. She walked ahead. Everyone went about their business not paying any mind to her. She was hit with a feeling at the bottom of her stomach. A feeling she had never felt before. The feeling was that of tardiness. Her pace quickened as the feeling grew stronger. Her walk morphed into a fast walk. Her fast walk matured into a jog. She saw a door at the end of the long hallway. She knew that's where she needed to go.

"Good luck, Nadia," Peter said as he sat in one of the waiting chairs.

She did not have time to acknowledge his well wishes or comprehend why he gave them.

Nadia quickly walked through the door and shut it behind her. There she saw a large wooden desk with a woman sitting behind it. The woman was entirely too small for such a desk. She seemed to be in her eighties. She was so thin it appeared as if someone had opened an air hole on her back and all of the air was released from her body. She wore old style eyeglasses that were kept on her face by two thin metallic strings that wrapped around her head. Her grey hair was done up in a bun. Without looking up from what she was reading, the woman reached for her wind up clock and placed it her viewing area.

"Four P.M. Precisely. On time. Muy Bien."

"Yes, I try to be," Nadia said quietly as she tried to mask her heavy breathing.

The woman looked up in Nadia's direction. Lines of concentration formed on her brow as she peered through her glasses.

"It is normal for an applicant to dress as they would if they were at the job he or she was applying for si?"

"Yes, Ma'am."

"And does your appearance ahora reflect your expectation on how you are to dress if you were to get the position?"

Nadia looked at her condition. Her white blouse was stained with a mixture of rain, sand, mustard, ketchup, and sweat. Her hair was a mess and her aroma was sickening. She did not know how to respond to the woman's question. She had no idea of what position she was even applying for. She was so intimidated by the small woman behind the large desk she dared not to ask. Instead she just stood there like a child who had been caught playing outside with their school clothes still on. The woman behind the desk eased the tension by letting off a giggle.

"I'm just giving you a hard time, Dear."

The woman then proceeded to let her hair out of a bun and let her grey hair fall down to her shoulders. She took her glasses of and stepped around the desk and sat on top of it facing Nadia.

"Everyone is in the same condition when they have orientation with Peter. I'm surprised he's in a decent condition himself," she said with a pleasant smile.

"You were a professor at Elyria State University si?"

"Yes, Ma'am."

"Muy Bien. Well you will do the same here at Escholar. That is the name of this suburb and it is the name of the university because the suburb is the university and the university is the suburb. My name is Helena Garcia. On Earth, you taught courses on religion. Here we call that history. Unfortunately, we already have a full staff of history teachers. We have assigned you to Earth Studies. You will teach students the ways of life on Earth. Here is your schedule. You will start in two weeks. That should give you plenty of time to get adjusted and situated. You will get the standard pay for professors here which you will find more than adequate for all of your needs. An advance will be placed in your Universal Monetary Account once you are situated. It is very good to have you with us Professor McKline."

"It's a pleasure to be here, Mrs. Garcia," Nadia said with a wide smile as she enthusiastically shook Mrs. Garcia's hand.

She was now beginning to feel apart of this place. She was going to be doing something she was so accustomed to. She was beginning to feel ok. She saw Peter standing there with his arm waiting for her.

"I didn't need any luck," she said laughing as she walked up to him.

Chapter 9

Nadia found herself gliding in a city of clouds at a quickened pace. It appeared as if the ground far beneath her was made of clouds. The vehicle that she and Peter were traveling on was a cloud itself. They were surrounded by hundreds of giant, light clouds. The top of the clouds were colored with white and a slight tint of gold. The bottoms were lined with a mixture of pink and blue. Some of the clouds looked as if they were lightly coated with sparkles. Neither Peter nor Nadia said a word as they traveled on their journey. Nadia closed her eyes and let the hot and relaxing air open the pores on her face and gently brush her hair back. She glanced down at the cloud in which they were traveling on. She was not sure what convinced her that this was ok, but she pinched a piece of the cloud and put it in her mouth. The warm morsel made her entire face come alive. She could feel a light tingling sensation in her teeth and gums. Her nostrils flared to inhale the hot air which filled her lungs and stimulated every nerve in her body. She looked over to find Peter looking at her enjoying her nibble of their transportation.

"Please try not to go overboard, Nadia. We do need this cloud to get to where we are going," Peter said mockingly.

As the collections of clouds began to dissipate, Nadia could see what was causing the beautiful reflection on the clouds. There were three suns positioned in the distant sky. There were two smaller ones that seemed to barely burn. In the middle of the two was an extremely large sun that burned brilliantly. The rays were intense, yet they needed no glasses or any eyewear to stare directly into it. It burned a golden color with light flashes of orange leaping off of its surface. Their cloud began to descend to the ground that seemed to be made of clouds. As they began to approach the surface, their cloud picked up its pace.

The hot air had suddenly become cool, and the angle of the cloud's decent seemed to get steeper and steeper. Nadia immediately began to have flashbacks of the plane crash. She began to scream at the top of her lungs but the gusting air pushed her cries back into her mouth and down her throat. Just when she thought it was the end all over again, their cloud blasted through the collection of clouds and into open air. Nadia then focused her eyes on perhaps the most beautiful setting she had ever seen.

They hovered over a large city that seemed to stretch forever. The buildings looked like golden reciprocated icicles. Each one had a different shape but most of them were long and thin like fingers. Various hues of gold flashed off of each one. In the center of the city was a much larger replica of the sand castle that the children had made on the beach in Dundon. It was shorter than the taller buildings but it occupied a larger portion of land. The top of the building reflected the light coming off the suns and matched their intensity. As they approached closer, they could see that the streets were not made of brick, or cement. The streets were made of a golden liquid. It was hard to tell if they were made of water because the reflection that was careening off of the buildings. It appeared to be too thick to be water, yet the many boats that rowed through it seemed to travel at ease. She looked around and saw that there seemed to be hundreds of thousands of clouds similar to theirs entering and leaving the city. There was also a large number of flying capsules that were entering and leaving as well. She saw roughly two hundred people flying through the air with no vehicles at all. She saw a flock of birds coming near them. She could see their beautiful long white wings as they flew in a "V" formation. As they flew closer, she could see that they were not birds at all. She could see the crowd of people as they flew by. The collection of men and women were made up of different races. Each one was in perfect physical condition and wore a stone straight face. They all wore helmets that seemed similar to cycling helmets. Each wore long white robes with backpacks. Each had a saber tucked near their side. Nadia instantly could tell what they were.

"Angels." She thought to herself.

Their vessel had descended enough to where they now mingled with the tops of the buildings. Nadia could now see the intricacies and precise craftsmanship of the structures that made up the city. The thin buildings appeared to be made of a combination of gold, silver and glass. The sidewalks were made of gold. The gold colored rivers which were the streets were next to the sidewalks but lowered 5 meters. Various small boats rowed slowly through the bright liquid. Children ran through the sidewalks and up stairs frolicking through the city. There was no vegetation around, everything was constructed yet it seemed to have a natural beauty.

When the cloud finally touched the ground, Nadia and Peter stepped off of it. Nadia could feel a current pass through her body as soon as her feet hit the golden sidewalk as if the ground was heated. Her eyes could not handle all of the beauty that was around her. The sun's rays reflecting off of the gold in the city and the golden river gave everything a golden hue. It was as if only shades of yellow existed with a few whites, and an occasional silver. Nadia fell to her knees and wept. She could feel comfort swelling in her heart being in this place. It was so much, she thought that perhaps her heart would burst and she would die all over again. After visiting the suburban areas she had her doubts. But those doubts were now eradicated. She was standing in the place that everyone had dreamed about. She could not stop the golden tears of joy from covering her face and running down her chin. She hid her bottom lip with her upper lip to prevent from yelling out what her heart was telling her. She felt like she was home despite being the farthest away from it. She did let her lips part for a brief moment. She could not help suppressing the one word that put everything into perspective. She did not let the word escape with a breath. She merely let her lips run through the motions of forming the word.

"Heaven."

"This is the main city," Peter informed her.

"As you can see it is quite different from the suburban areas surrounding the city. This city has no name. Many people know it by many different names. The name does not matter. The fact that you are here is all that matters. Many of these buildings are off limits to citizens. You must get authorization to enter certain buildings. You need not worry about that because there will never be a reason to go in any of them. There are resting areas for lunches and hotels to stay in for vacations. It's quite an entertaining place if you want more sophisticated entertainment than what Urbanopolis has to offer. The winged people you saw gliding in the clouds are soldiers. They will protect us from terrorism from the other side. We have yet to have a terrorist attack, but I'm sure you're aware of the other side I'm talking about and what they are capable of. You know of the final war that will take place. But not to worry, our army is well prepared."

Peter lightly grabbed Nadia by the arm and pulled her close. He came as close as he could to her ear without kissing it. In the lightest octave he could muster he reiterated the most important rule of all.

"You must never enter these buildings. The ones for entertainment are clearly marked. Never enter those which are not. If I were you I would not even enter the theaters, or museums. It's ok to stay in hotels but that's about it."

Peter added more distance between himself and Nadia. The intense expression on his face regressed to his usual goofy look.

"Well you have seen all seven cities. Now you must choose which city you would like to live in."

Before Nadia could respond with an answer she found herself standing in the living room of a quaint apartment. The floor was covered with a beige carpet. Despite the dim lighting, Nadia could tell that the walls were white. On one of the walls was a modern style fireplace with its casing trimmed with gold. She looked around and detected where the kitchen area was.

"You have one bedroom and a dining area in one of the other rooms," Peter informed her.

"Your financial information is in your account. All you need to use for purchases is your thumb. In your bedroom, on your dresser you will find a cell phone for you to use. The apartment here is furnished with a home phone. My cell phone number is programmed into both. You have a full wardrobe in the closet that you will find to your liking. The refrigerator is stocked with all of your favorite foods. I think everything is covered. Do you have any other questions?"

"My husband. Where does he live?"

"I wish I could help you with that question. He was not assigned to me. You also must consider the fact that he may not be here with us on this side."

Nadia would not let the prospect of never seeing her love again. Deep in her heart she could feel him out there. She was convinced she would see him again.

"He's on this side. How do I find him?"

"Well you chose the right city, Escholar . There is the Building of Records on Main Street. There is a collection of most of the people here. There are many systems and it will take a lot of searching to find people. You may get lucky and find him immediately."

"I will do whatever it takes."

"Good. Well I will be on my way. You need to get some rest. If you need anything give me a call. Good luck with everything."

"Thank you, Peter. Thank you for everything," Nadia said with the greatest appreciation.

"I'm just doing my job, Nadia," Peter said with a silly grin.

"Hey Peter. Wait a sec. Earlier you said that we visited seven cities. We only saw six."

"Good night Nadia."

As soon as he left, Nadia immediately shed herself of the disgusting clothes and jumped in a hot shower. She enjoyed the hot water cleansing her of her busy day.

Nadia closed her eyes. In her mind she tried to imagine Tyson standing behind her as he always did. She imagined that her hand was his lathering her shoulders letting the suds flow down her arms. She then wrapped her hands around herself and attempted to hold herself as he did. Her hands rubbed the opposing arms in a comforting way. She began to lightly dance back and forth. Her head was tilted to the left to meet his that was normally on that shoulder. Her hands lightly caressed her soft belly and hips. She would take time to lightly grip her hips. They were not her hands tonight, but his. She let a single finger lightly lower itself down until it hit its target. When she found it, she let out a sigh. She could feel an explosion in her stomach ready to erupt as her finger continued to work. There was an explosion but it was not from her stomach. It was from her heart and the eruption happened through her eyes. Reality had struck her. She was dead. He was not there. The pain of not having him there surpassed her impending pleasure. Nadia sank in the shower as she began to cry. She sat in the shower in a balled position crying as hard as she could. She did not care about disturbing the neighbors. She wanted everyone to hear her pain. If she did not find her man, she would implode. She knew she would find him, but that did not remedy her at the moment. In the moment, she was alone. Void of love and affection that he provided her with every night.

When Nadia was finished crying, she sat motionless. The hot water continued beating against her head and shoulders. Her eyes were outlined with redness. She did not blink and she did not close her mouth. She didn't think. She just sat there.

When Nadia finally pulled herself together, she stepped out of the shower and dried herself off. She put on some comfortable pajamas that were in one of her drawers. She crawled in her king size bed and underneath her blankets. She went to lean over only to find a cold empty spot. She would have begun crying again but her body was drained of any liquid that would be used for tears. She slowly pulled back her arm and held it to her side. Before she knew it, she was fast asleep.

Chapter 10

Over time, Nadia grew more comfortable with her surroundings, but not with having Tyson being absent of those surroundings. Her thoughts were on him at all times of the day except when she was teaching classes in Escholar. Each day she would get up; fix herself a small breakfast and workout in the gym that was on the fifth floor of the apartment complex. When she was finished with her workout, she would get ready for work. Teaching was the only link she had back to Earth. It was the only time of the day she actually smiled. She loved her students. Some of them were her former students from Earth. When she wasn't teaching, she was over at the Building of Records. This was the most frustrating part of the day for Nadia. The building was a modern building and the information system seemed to be advanced in technology. The actual record keeping was a farce. The entire system was made of smaller systems. Each system had only two search options. There was First Name and Last Name. The database would then produce a table that had a list of names, addresses, times of death, and who their case worker was. A single name could result in millions of returns. The fields could be sorted by any of the categories but that only helped a little. Another problem was how people were filed. There were systems based on creed, location on Earth, century of birth, cause of death, age of death, and marital status. These information systems did not cross reference one another. Someone could be in one database but not the other despite qualifying for both. Nadia spent all of her evenings looking through databases and files eagerly searching records. The lack of sleep began to pull down her face. The edges of her eyes matched her hair color. Her red lips began to fade pink.

Every once in a while curiosity would get the best of Nadia. To relieve her eyes from looking at the

same name for hours and hours, she would put a
different name to search.

Ghandi.

Name not found.

Martin King.

Name not found.

Anne Frank.

Name not found.

The results gave Nadia the chills. She had a
mental list of the influential people she wanted to talk
to when she made it to Heaven. She never did think of
the fact that those people may have done things in their
private lives that would prevent them from entering
paradise. When she thought of this, Peter's grave
words echoed in her head.

"You also must consider the fact that he may
not be here with us on this side."

When that statement infiltrated her thoughts,
she knew it was time to quit searching for the day. She
would retreat to her usual spot in a park underneath an
apple tree and have a small snack before heading
home. This particular park was on a raised hill which
allowed her to get a great view of Escholar. Looking
at all of the historic looking buildings from the

different time periods relaxed her. They were so contrasting to one another yet they fit in Escholar.

One particular evening, Peter's words seemed to play at a louder volume in her mind than normal. When she arrived at her spot underneath the apple tree in the park she found that the words followed her there. She tried to eat her tuna sandwich, some of the apples available to her, or one of her cubes of cheese but she found her appetite had vanished. Those words had stolen it. Nadia sat there. At that moment, she felt totally helpless. Her heart could not bear the rationale that her mind was feeding it. She could not survive without him, even in paradise. The fact that it was paradise made it that much worse. When Peter first broke the news to her about Peter as she lay in the hospital bed, she was devastated, but she thought she could die herself and see him again. Now there is no dying again. There is no hoping for the next stage. This was the final stage and he was gone. Nadia began to partake in her favorite hobby since arriving, crying. She cried in the shower. She cried in her sleep. This time she had no intention of stopping.

"The salt in your tears will soil your fruit. Some people like to sprinkle a little salt on their fruit.

Some people wash their fruit to make sure only the true flavor of the fruit is there. Washing and adding salt to fruit doesn't make any sense so there is no use crying over your fruit."

Nadia wiped the tears from her eyes and looked up from the apple she was squeezing in her hand. She saw a woman standing over her. She seemed rather short. She wore an old brown baseball cap. Small tips of blonde hair stuck out just enough from the cap to tell the woman had extremely short hair. She wore thin eyeglasses that rested over her brown eyes. The woman flashed a simple smile that was flawed with a couple of misguided teeth but nevertheless possessed the brilliance to immediately lighten Nadia's mood. She wore a navy blue sweater with the letters U.S.A. embroidered on the front in brown letters. She also wore tan khaki shorts and brown sandals. Despite the baggy sweater, Nadia could tell that this young woman had slightly broad athletic shoulders. In spite of the hiking apparel, short hair, and the total absence of makeup, this woman had a feminine grace to her.

"May I have a seat?"

Nadia welcomed the woman to sit down and have lunch with her. Before having a seat, the woman selected a few of the giant green apples from the tree and had a seat next to Nadia. There was something comforting about the young woman that put Nadia at ease. Her demeanor was very smooth and fluid. It felt like somehow this woman was family. It could have been from her smile. It could have been because Nadia did not have the opportunity to have someone to experience girl talk with.

"May I ask your name?"

"My name is Beth."

"I hope you don't mind me asking, but what's your last name?"

"No last name. Just Beth. It's a pleasure to meet you, Nadia."

Nadia had forgotten to ask her why she not had a last name because the question she did ask was going to solve something that was more bizarre.

"How did you know my name?"

"Oh, I'm sorry to scare you. I don't want you to think that I'm crazy or anything. The security guard that signs everyone in and out always says goodbye to you."

Both of the women looked at one another and began to laugh. For Nadia, it was a sigh of relief. For the first time since arriving, something she found strange actually had a reasonable explanation.

"So what is his name?"

"And how do you know I'm looking for a man?" Nadia asked jokingly.

"Well for starters you are there everyday. Secondly, when you leave there everyday your eyes are as fiery as your hair, and your forehead is wrinkled and you leave in a hurry. Hell, you didn't even know the security guard said goodbye to you everyday."

Once again, both women shared a good laugh. A few tears escaped from Nadia. Her reason for laughing was also her burden.

"His name is Tyson. I miss him so much."

Nadia wiped away her newly born tears.

"I will find him," Nadia said with a determined spirit. Beth took her hand for support.

"We are going to be together again. I look forward to sharing some of the wonderful things here with him. I look forward to sitting under this tree and hear with him eating apples off this very tree. We are going to be happy together forever. That's when Heaven will actually start feeling like Heaven."

"When you find Tyson you won't be eating apples under this tree," Beth said that caused more laughter.

"I'm sorry. I'm rambling on and on. What about you? What's the name of the man you're looking for?"

"I'm actually looking for a man and a woman. My parents."

"When did they die?" Nadia asked Beth.

"I don't know. I never knew my parents. Ever since I was a very little girl I've lived here, away from Earth I mean. I grew up in a local orphanage with other children my age. The only things I know about Earth is from what I've read from books. What a crazy place. I'm not sure if my parents are still on Earth or if one or the other is here. Because I'm not sure if they are on Earth or not, it's hard to know if I'm looking for nothing."

"There is also the possibility that they are not on this side," Nadia said in a straightforward way.

"Oh my, you must have Peter as your counselor," Beth said laughing which caused Nadia to follow with laughter of her own.

"Do you know when you died?

"No. I haven't found anything yet. I'm not sure if I even died at all. All I know is that I just exist."

This time, Nadia clutched Beth's hand as a sign of encouragement.

"I'm sorry that you have to go through this."

"Don't be. From what I hear of Earth I am happy because of the things I didn't go through," Beth said with a mocking laugh.

"I feel sorry that you had to go through what you had to," Beth said with a smile.

"As much as I look forward to finally meeting my parents, that is the easier of my two problems."

"What is the other problem?"

"Finding my girl," Beth answered as she lowered her head and softened her tone.

"Oh you have a daughter?"

"No. My girlfriend."

The women had finished their lunches, stood up and began to walk down the street.

"Where did you meet your girlfriend?" Nadia asked.

"We met at a club in Urbanopolis. It was funny because I was on a date with another woman at the time. It was a real small smoke filled night club. I was with my date sitting at one of the booths having a drink. I could feel a set of eyes holding onto me. I finally saw where this feeling was coming from. A few tables down sat a tall, slender woman. Her straight blonde hair was just long enough to give her shoulders a light kiss. She would only take her brown eyes off of me for a second to say something to the group of women she was with and then they were right back on me. My gut feeling told me that her and her friends were making fun of my date and I. My date didn't notice at all, but I sure did. Normally I can turn a blind eye towards ignorance but it was something about this woman's brown eyes. As the night went on, her stare got more intense and more serious. Her facial expressions even hinted toward violent intent. There was a point in the night when my date left to use the restroom. I was there alone in the nightclub with this group of women constantly staring and laughing. I was finished taking their non verbal insults. I was going to walk up to the group and let them know if they had planned on doing something to my date and I, now was the time to do it. As I began to walk closer to the group, the tall blonde began to walk towards me. We exchanged angry looks as the distance between us shrank. Finally we got close enough to each other to let our words fly. With a bad attitude, I asked her what her problem was. She then fired the question right back at me. She then told me if I had a problem with a group of lesbians sitting together having a good time, we could settle it right then and there. I asked her to run that by me again. I was totally confused. She then told me that she had noticed me staring at her and her group with a mean look that she didn't like. I then informed her that she was the one that started with the glares towards my date and I and that was the only reason I stared back. She sarcastically apologized for finding me attractive and giving a few glances. She stopped herself to ask if that was really my date. This time around, it was her that was shocked. I then told her again that the woman I was with was indeed my date. The tense look on her faced eased up. She apologized for staring and told me that she would not have been staring so hard if she knew that was my girlfriend. I let her know that the woman I was with wasn't my girlfriend but a blind date. The woman then gave a small laugh. She told me that everything up to that point had been a total embarrassment and anything that happens after that couldn't be any more embarrassing. She told me her name was Mary. She then grabbed my hand and wrote her number on my hand. She then told me to give her a call if things didn't work out with my blind date. She turned to walk away. Before she rejoined her friends, she turned around and moved her lips to say something that I couldn't hear but I could understand. She told me to have a bad night. The night was actually nice until my blind date found the number written on my palm at the end of the date. The next day I gave Mary a call. I figured if this number was going to cost me a woman, it should be for a good reason. That day we met for lunch at a small café in Dundon. It was magic ever since. We dated for two years. Those were my best two years. I felt like someone loved me. Don't get me wrong, I received a lot of care and attention growing up in the orphanage, but this was different. I was one of many children special to the staff. With Mary, I alone was special to her. She was someone I could have all to myself and vice versa. As soon as we started talking about marriage, it all changed. One day I came back to our apartment from class, and the door was opened. I walked to find the apartment trashed. The coffee table was overturned. There were papers and feathers from the couch pillows peppered all over the place. I yelled out for Mary, but she never did answer. Instead I was approached by one of the soldiers that look like what you would call an angel on Earth. I asked him what was going on. He told me that Mary had been arrested. I asked him what was the charge and he told me told me that it was her and her family's personal business. He then asked if I was a sister or cousin. I told him no and he went searching in the other room. I wasn't sure, but I suspected it was because she was a lesbian so I ran out of the apartment before they could figure things out. I returned a few hours later to straighten up but they never came for me. The more I thought about it, the more I was certain her sexual orientation was the reason. The funny thing is, they never came for me. If she was guilty of that supposed sin, so was I. Maybe she was arrested for something else. It was so hard not having her there. Not having her sleeping next to me. I even still make breakfast for two. Well I decided to stop sulking and do something about it. I went to see a lawyer. After talking to a lawyer, he made me see that I was in quite the conundrum. See, if I was still here and I was innocent, she was innocent and should be brought back from the other side. If she is guilty, then so am I and I will be sent to the other side. By pursuing this, I can either get my love back or condemn myself. I am willing to take the chance so I am always in the main city looking through records and documents to find a way to get her back."

Nadia noticed that Beth's breathing rate increased rapidly since the beginning of her story. Her face was pale and she was shaking. Nadia gave her a hug. Beth soaked Nadia's shoulder with her lonely tears. Beth's tears resembled same tears that Nadia had been producing since arriving. Both women stood up and brushed the crumbs off of themselves. They thanked each other for their support and went to their homes. On the way back, Nadia smiled to herself. She thought of how nice it was to have a friend. She now had a friend that understood her plight. Beth's situation seemed worse than hers. Beth knew where her love was and that was on the other side suffering. Not only did she have to deal with that, but if she was not careful, she would be suffering also.

Nadia had arrived at the front door of her apartment complex. She walked through the glass doors and into the main lobby.

"Nadia I have something for you," the desk attendant said.

Nadia walked over and he handed her an envelope. She did not bother opening it until she was upstairs and inside of her apartment. She set the envelope down on the coffee table in the living room so she could take off her coat. She came back inside the living room and picked it up. Only her name was written on the front of the envelope. She opened it up and read the note inside.

"I cannot believe I've found you. I miss you so much. Come to the First Hotel in the Main City tomorrow night at ten o'clock. I miss you.

Love, Your Husband."

Chapter 11

Nadia looked at the First Hotel from her water taxi. Despite the late hour of ten o'clock, the three suns still touched the sky, buildings, water, sidewalks and people with their golden fingers, magically giving every object a golden hue. She stepped off of the water taxi and took the escalator up to the sidewalk level. Once at the top, Nadia found herself directly in front of the hotel. She stopped to think for a moment about what awaited her inside. Inside was the love she had missed so much. She had somewhat enjoyed paradise up to this point, but she knew when the night was over, things would seem much sweeter.

Nadia walked through the revolving glass doors that sparkled as the rotating glass volleyed the sun's rays between one another. The lobby had gold and white colored marble on the floor. There was a desk for an attendant, but no one was there. No one was in the lobby at all. She was alone with an elevator. She walked up to the elevator and pressed the up arrow.

Instantly the silver doors opened. On the floor of the
elevator, was a silver tray. The tray held a single white
candle, a room key, a red rose, and a note. Nadia
stepped into the elevator. She picked up the candle
and went to blow it out, but it immediately
extinguished itself. She sat the candle down and
picked up the room key and note. The note was blank.
The room key did not have a number to it. She then
realized that the elevator was inclining without her
knowing where it would stop. Tonight she cared not
for reason, only for love. She would ride the elevator
to the three suns if it were to deliver her to love.

The elevator stopped on the floor it chose and
the silver doors opened. Nadia stepped out of the
elevator and into a hallway. The carpet was a burned
orange color and the walls were white. There were no
pictures, fire extinguishers, or vending machines. The
only thing that was in the hallway at all beside the
elevator was a single room door. There were no other
rooms on that floor. Nadia walked toward the door
and went to open the door but just as she went to
clutch the handle, the door opened on its own.

Nadia thought she had opened the doorway to
space. All she could see was calm darkness. The only

thing that gave her any sense of the direction was the trail that was laid out in front of her that led to into the darkness. The trail consisted of lines of small glass vases that could fit in the palm of her hand. Inside each vase was a clear liquid. Small white flowers rested atop of the liquid. The vases were illuminated by a small white flame that was lit at the center of each flower. Two rows of vases formed a path. Nadia eased the toe of her shoe in the center of the pathway to make sure she did not fall into an eternal void. She found that her foot could rest on a surface she could not see. Feeling more confident, she took another step unit she was now fully standing on the path. She began walking down the path. She stopped to turn to see how far she had walked from the door only to find the door was now gone. One meter down the path, she arrived at a white curtain that appeared to hang from nothing. To her right, there was a white dress that seemed to hang from the darkness. It was a dress that seemed to be from ancient roman times. The dress had a plunging neckline and tapered slightly at the waist. The bottom was long and flowing to the ankles. Nadia took off her business attire and put on the dress that was a perfect fit. Tyson never did get her size right, but this time it seemed as if he put a little more effort into his purchase. To Nadia's left, there was a small table with a mirror. She picked up the white hair brush and went to put up her hair. As she went to grab a handful of her hair, she discovered her hair was already put up. She sat down the brush on the table, and sat herself down at the table. She saw there was makeup placed in front of her. She looked in the mirror to apply the makeup and saw that her hair was now the color white and her eyes were sky blue. This stunned her for a short time, but she proceeded to apply the makeup. She continued to apply the lipstick, mascara, and blush despite it not showing up on her face.

Once Nadia was finished preparing herself, the white curtain opened. She found another path in darkness was laid at her feet. This path was identical to the first, but this time the small flower that was inside each vase was now yellow. The flame inside of each flower now had a golden hue. Nadia began to walk down the path until she arrived at a yellow wall of beads. Nadia walked through the beads to find she was standing on a yellow tiled floor. In the center of the tile was a yellow wood grained table. Nadia walked over to the table and sat down in the matching chair. As soon as she sat down she heard a harp strumming in the far distance. A voice of a woman singing could be heard all around. The voice was so soft, that Nadia could not decipher what language it was. There was no way of telling where the light song was emanating from. The table was decorated with an assortment of yellow flowers. There was a single yellow candle in the center of the table. Directly in front of her was a large silver platter. Nadia stared into the shiny platter find that her appearance was altered. Her hair was now blonde. Her eyes were now green. Her dress was now yellow. The makeup that failed to apply now gave her skin a naturally tan glow. She removed the top of the platter to uncover what was to be her meal. On her plate was a chicken breast that was glazed with a yellow sauce. The main dish was accompanied by a side of corn and buttered noodles. There was a golden glass that contained pineapple zinfandel. Nadia picked up her knife and fork and cut into the tender golden meat on her plate. She stabbed a sliver that she had cut free and placed it in her mouth. She immediately closed her eyes and took a deep breath as she savored the morsel she chewed. The piece of chicken was so delicious; a line of saliva escaped her mouth. She washed it down with the yellow libation that rested in her golden cup. Tyson was never a great cook. The meal was surely prepared by someone else. That was the only explanation. The other things that were taking place had no reasonable explanation. She did not care. From her time in the afterlife she realized that it was best to just go along with things the way they were. She thought of all the trouble Tyson went through to put this together. Tyson was romantic in a spontaneous way. He definitely kept her on her toes. He was not romantic in a sweet way and this was definitely sweet.

Nadia began to reminisce when she first spent the night at his apartment. She would wake up to a burning aroma that filled the air. She arose from her twisted position which was caused by Tyson's rickety twin size bed. She would throw on one of his many soccer jerseys and her panties and headed over to the kitchen area of the apartment.

"What are you doing? What is that awful smell?" she would ask him in a raspy, morning voice as she wiped the sleep from her eyes.

"I'm making you a grand breakfast. A special breakfast just for you."

"If this grand breakfast you're cooking is a reflection of how you feel about me, maybe I shouldn't have stayed the night last night," she would say laughing.

Tyson walked over to her and sat her at his small table. He then proceeded to set plates holding various breakfast foods. They were supposed to be breakfast foods. The eggs were runny, the toast was scorched, and the oatmeal was pasty.

"Honey, I know you tried, but let me cook us something that we can actually eat."

Tyson then proceeded to serve himself with all of the dishes he had cooked. He took his fork and filled it with a sample from the eggs and oatmeal that were on his plate. Nadia attempted to bring him back to his senses before he ate the food.

"As I said before, this is a grand breakfast. I made it out of the care and the love that I have for you. I tried my best, and put my heart and soul into it. I know the toast is burned, and the eggs aren't perfect. The oatmeal will most likely make me sick for the rest of the day. Like our relationship, I'm willing to accept the mistakes and errors as long as they are done with care and love. For the love of you, I gladly eat my mistakes."

Tyson then proceeded to eat the food that rested on his fork and refilled it for a second bite. Nadia's eyes filled with tears of affection as she filled her plate with food and also ate for the love of Tyson.

Nadia had finished the food that was on her plate and took the last sip of zinfandel that was in her golden glass. She took her yellow napkin and wiped away the tears that filled her eyes.

Nadia looked to her left and saw another trail. This was the same as its two predecessors, only this time the theme was blue. Even the flames in the center of the tiny flowers were blue. Already accustomed to the procedure, Nadia took her one meter walk down the path until she arrived at a blue cloud of smoke. Nadia stepped through the cloud and found herself standing in a room with a marble floor that was a combination of the colors sky blue and dark blue. The walls and ceiling were covered with the same surface in which the floor was covered. On the opposite end of the room were four giant pillars that were also made of the same material the walls and floor. In the center of the pillars, the floor was raised by two steps that let do a circular object. As Nadia walked closer to it, she could hear what it was meant for. She could hear the racing water and see the dancing steam that came from the hot tub. Inside, the water was not clear, but a blue that resembled blueberry juice. Blue jagged gems were visible through the translucent liquid by their reflecting shine.

Nadia lifted her blue dress over her head and set it on the floor. She made sure that every blue hair was placed back in position so not one would get wet. She walked up the two steps and sat down over the hot tub with her feet lightly pressing on the surface. She lightly kicked the light blue rose petals along the water with her left large toe. Slowly she began to lower herself in the hot water which made every hair vibrate with pleasure. Nadia was fully immersed in the liquid except for her head. She did not want to ruin her blue lipstick, eye shadow, and blush by wetting her face. As soon as her skin came in contact with the tiny gems, they instantly began to vibrate causing Nadia to let out a sigh of comfort. Nadia leaned her head back against the edge of the hot tub and watched the rose petals sail along the blue water.

One of the petals resembled a sailing boat she and Tyson used during a vacation. The petal sailed away on its own just as they did that day. She remembered gliding along the water, watching him maneuver the boat until they found a piece of the lake that was absolutely calm. She stood up as Tyson dropped a rope and gave him a huge hug and kiss. He then stepped behind her and with his long arms, wrapped her and held her close. They both looked at the setting sun that was ready to be extinguished by the lake's horizon.

"This is heaven. I wish every day could be like this."

"Nadia, everyday is like this."

"I don't recall being on a beautiful lake in a boat watching the sunset. Maybe the lazy students in my class and the snow blurred my memory."

Tyson then turned Nadia around and massaged her cheeks with his thumbs.

"I am with you now as I was yesterday. You said this is heaven. For me, everyday is heaven when I'm with you."

She stood on her toes and pressed his head down to meet hers at the lips. He squeezed her hips into his as they shared a passionate kiss.

"Baby are you as hot as I am right now?" Tyson asked with a devilish smile.

"I think I'm hot as I've ever been right now," Nadia replied kissing on his chest.

"How about a swim?" Tyson said as he pushed her into the lake.

Nadia could picture herself falling in the cool lake with laughter on her face. As soon as she saw herself submerge in the lake, she was instantly taken back to the day of the plane crash. She could see the arms, legs, eyes and other body parts flying across her in the water that was tainted with blood. Dead babies appeared to reanimate and cry out for her help. Nadia looked at the bottom of the water and saw the half face of Tyson calling out to her for help.

Nadia quickly jumped from the blue water and tumbled over the two steps that led to the hot tub. She was up just as quick as she had fallen down. She took a moment to compose herself as she stared at the hot tub.

Nadia saw a blue stand to her left. A blue towel rested on the stand. She picked it up to use it to dry off. Before she began she was already dry. She walked over and slipped on her dress. As soon as she was dressed, she saw another trail. This time the accent was red. Each tiny flower in the glass jars held a bright red flame. Nadia took her one meter stroll down the path.

At the end of the path, Nadia found a single red wooden door. She went to open the door but as she went to grab the handle, the door opened itself. Past the door was a vintage French style bedroom. There was a canopy bed that was covered in a light red cloth. The satin bedding was pink with red pillows. A large window with long red curtains was located to the right of the bed. Oversized pink and red rose petals rained down from the ceiling covering the floor as well as everything in the room. The light red cloth spared the bed from the sprinkling petals. To the left there was a dresser with a giant mirror. Nadia gazed at herself in the mirror. Her hair color had returned to its natural auburn color. Her eyes were once again light brown. Her lipstick was a dark red. Her blush gave her cheeks a rosy hue. Looking through the mirror, Nadia spotted lingerie hanging on a hanger on the opposite side of the room. She walked over to where it was hanging. She went to take off the red dress to put on the lingerie. When she went to take off the dress she found that the lingerie was on her body. She looked back up at the hanger and it was bare. Nadia moved back over to the mirror. She looked at herself in the lingerie. The non existent neckline on the sheer see through top enhanced her bust which needed no help. The bottom of the top stopped at just her navel and did not reach the dark red satin panties. She tried to pull on the bottom of the top but a light whisper in the air stopped her.

"You are beautiful".

Nadia walked over to the bed and sat at its foot. She immediately felt something underneath her. She stood up and found she had sat on a sleeping mask. She raised her hands to let down her hair, but before they reached their destination, her hair fell and rested on her shoulders. She lifted the mask over her head and slipped it over her hair and onto her face. She found that it fit perfectly over eyes.

Nadia stood perfectly still in complete darkness. With her eyes shielded, all of her other senses intensified. She could taste the apple and cinnamon fragrance in the air. She could feel the slight warm breeze flowing from the window run through her lingerie. She could hear the falling rose petals chat amongst themselves as they collected on one another. She even could taste the cherry lipstick that was on her face.

Nadia was startled by warm air on her neck. Two soft hands lightly gripped her shoulders and turned her around. The two hands then pushed themselves through her hair. She continued to remain perfectly still. She felt a nose press against the tip of hers. Another current of warm air was omitted from the nostrils and onto her lips. The muscles in her body were awakening and she could feel her extremities once again. She put her hands on a man's chest and moved her fingers up to his neck, around to his ears, and over his face. The tips of her fingers were moistened by tears. Nadia felt her face heat up with emotion as she began to cry. Before she could let out one wail, her lips were sealed with his. The touch of his lips and tenderness of his arms were strong enough to suppress her tears. She slowly maneuvered her fingers through his hair. She was surprised to discover

that his hair was shorter than she anticipated. Tyson
had always kept his long shaggy hair. He also seemed
much shorter than he was on Earth. He even smelled
and tasted different as she pecked at his neck. She
thought perhaps he decided to change his appearance.
He didn't need to. To her, Tyson was a beautiful statue
come to life. She did not care what he had changed
about his physical appearance. It was him. It was her
husband. The man she had spent so long searching for
in paradise was now with her. She knew it was him
from his touch. He knew all of her pleasure zones and
how she liked to be touched. He knew to lightly
massage her hips. She liked that because he loved the
parts of her body that she did not. When he grazed the
back of his fingernails across the backside of her panty
line, it made every hair on her body stand at attention.
His mouth made its way down to her neck and he
gently gripped her skin with his lips. She moaned and
stroked the back of his neck letting him know she
appreciated it. She motioned her hands up to the mask
to remove it to see what he looked like. Before she
could take it off, his hands tightly grabbed her wrists
sending a reaction of fear all over her body. She stood
frozen as the soft hands kept their aggressive hold on

her wrists. With the grip still in place, the hands pulled her entire body close to his until she was close enough to receive a long, slow kiss. The hands lowered her hands to the bottom of his shirt. Once she grabbed his shirt the grip was released. She raised the bottom of his shirt up over his head and away from his arms. She eliminated the space between them once again and continued to kiss him. Despite her top, the dance that both of their nipples shared began to excite her in every way. She lowered her hands to his belt and did away with it. She then unzipped his pants and with one motion forced his pants and boxers down. She slid her finger nails up his thigh and lightly held him in her hand.

"Yep, it's still the same," she thought to herself.

He walked towards her despite no room which caused her to fall back on the bed. She could feel his hands going up her legs and around her waist. Her panties were then removed. She then felt the heat from his bare body hovering over hers and she felt her top fly away. His fingers ran through her hair like a fork through spaghetti. He twirled and flipped her shoulder length red locks. His hands then ran over her forehead and over her face, playing close attention to her nose, cheeks and mouth. He then gave her forehead a long kiss. He followed that kiss with a succession of kisses on both of her cheeks and nose. He then stopped and gave her mouth a light, tender kiss.

Nadia could not believe how sweet and gentle Tyson had become. He was paying such close attention to her reactions whenever he touched and kissed her. She always enjoyed being intimate with him but not in this way. He was always wild and rough. He would pleasure her by getting her heart rate accelerated. This Tyson was pleasuring her by relaxing her. He was making her feel as if there was no such things as space and time. She felt there was nothing in the world but them and she did not care.

His mouth moved down, gave her chin a brush and over to her ears where he gave her light flickers of his tongue. From there he worked his way down to her neck where he began sucking hard on her flesh. Her torso began swaying to the left and right. She rubbed his back up and down vigorously. Her hands then moved down to his buttocks to press him as close to her as she could manage. Despite her uncontrollable anticipation, he kept his slow, methodical pace. He worked his way to her neck with a long lick, to the center of her chest. With both of his hands he gently cupped her full breasts massaging their sides. He kissed around the left breast and slowly worked his tongue around the sides until he came to the top. He gave the nipple a hard tug with his lips that released a loud moan that originated from Nadia's stomach. Once the left nipple was to a point, he slowly worked his tongue over to the right side and gave the right breast the identical attention. Once both nipples were identical, he gave a long lick down from the center of her breasts down ill he reached her belly button. He gave her belly button a few licks and kisses which made her legs lock tightly around his back. He then began to give multiple kisses to her perspiring skin as he worked his way down. Nadia began to shake and moan as he reached her shaven pubic region. He gave light kisses around the edges. Nadia tried to direct his head where it needed to be but he refused. He gave her a light graze with his nose. The anticipation was too much for Nadia to handle. Just as she thought he was ready to give her what she wanted. His mouth began to kiss its way back to her thigh and down to her leg. He was taking her on a trip to insanity. He made his

way to her toes as he gave each one oral attention. He
then proceeded to guide his way back up to her leg and
up her thigh. He went up to her belly button giving it a
kiss and up between her breasts stopping at each nipple
back to her mouth as he gave her another long kiss.
She did not receive the treatment she wanted but she
was ready for the next step. She tried to guide his hips
over hers, but once again he refused to allow her to
take control of his body. Instead, he continued to kiss
her. She wanted to bite his tongue in frustration but
she dared not. He then worked his way back down
between her breasts, stopping at each nipple, down to
her belly button giving it a lick, down to her hips and
right back where she wanted him. Once again he gave
her a little nudge with his nose. She tried with all of
her might to get him to commit, but he kept at his pace.
He gave her a closed mouth kiss as if he were kissing
her face. He would pull away and repeat the same
procedure. He finally let his tongue stretch out and
gave her a long slow lick. Nadia let out a giant moan
as her legs began to shake beyond her control. His
licks increasingly intensified as they came at a quicker
pace and went deeper. Nadia's body wildly tossed
around as she screamed as loud as she could. Tiny

explosions went off in her stomach. She finally exploded. She exploded from her mouth, in her heart, in her mind and on him. She was ready to float right off of the bed. He stopped and moved his way back over her. He kissed her once more. He laid himself over her as she raised her legs and hips. He tortured her once more by rubbing himself over her but never inserting himself. Her hips began to rock up and down until he finally brought them together. She took a huge gasp as her eyes opened wide underneath the sleeping mask. Her senses all went numb except for her lower extremities as he took long, deep and slow strokes. She could not feel herself breathing. As he picked up his pace she could feel her heart keep up with his pace. She could not even hear herself scream as loud as she had ever screamed. He continued to kiss her and stroke her hair with his hand. When she climaxed, she could not even feel her lower extremities. Only her mind was there and it was barely functioning. This was the first time Heaven felt like heaven.

Nadia woke up the next morning still blinded by the sleeping mask. She removed it with no restriction. She looked down and saw a bare arm around her waist. He was sleeping behind her. She took a giant breath of the air that came in from the open window. The sweet music the birds outside sang convinced her to relax and lay down. She did not bother to see Tyson's new look. There was eternity for that. For now, there was only rest. When she felt him waking up behind him, she grabbed his hand and pushed herself back on him.

"I missed you so much," she told him.

"I missed you too. It feels like it has been forever."

Nadia knew that voice. She could never forget it. But it did not belong to Tyson.

Chapter 12

Nadia whirled around in the bed to find herself extremely close to a man with a short length, neat and sophisticated hair style. His sky blue eyes looked back at her.

"Nadia."

"Brenden."

Brenden was Nadia's first husband. He was the first love her life. Her thoughts instantly took her back to when they first met. It was during a rally at Elyria State University when it was a community college. It was her second year on campus and he was finishing his Bachelor's with a state university on campus. She was in the main square located in the center of the campus when a gust of wind carried her folder that contained her midterm paper for her sociology class. All she could do is watch helplessly as her two week long dedication to higher learning drifted towards the drain. Instantly, her hero dashed into the swirling water sacrificing his wardrobe for her work. She saw the half soaked gentleman step out of the water with her work protected by her folder.

"Here you are Ma'am," he said with a gentle smile.

"You must be some sort of idiot to get soaked for a folder with a few sheets of paper in it."

"Well I do know that it is that time of the semester and I think what is in this folder is more than just mere sheets of paper. Besides, I've been waiting for the perfect opportunity to introduce myself."

That would have been the worst line she would have ever heard if it were indeed a line. She looked in his sky blue eyes and saw sincerity reflected back towards her. She could see by the fading smile that he was taking her silence as disinterest.

"Hello my name is…"

"Nadia," he said finishing her sentence.

"Wow, you really have been noticing me," she said blushing.

"Yes, from a distance. I got your name from the front of your folder."

The both shared their first laugh.

"My name is Brenden. Brenden Scalloway. It is a pleasure to finally meet you Nadia."

That night they made arrangements to have drinks at a local pub across the street from the campus. As time went on, the meetings at the pub became a regular event. She was impressed by the aura of calm that radiated from him. He was always the classic gentleman. He was always standing when she stood, opening doors, carrying her books, taking her jacket and even conceding to her for evening plans. He was a father's dream, yet he was not boring in the least bit. His subtle humor constantly gave her stomach a light workout. They also talked about what they wanted to do with their lives. He told her of his aspirations to work for an accounting firm for a few years until he was able to start his own firm. She confessed her intentions to do something in the field of religion. Most people scoffed at those plans but he supported her. It was he who convinced her that she could utilize her dream in the educational field. She could feel love taking her over. She felt it each time they hugged. She felt it each time he gave her a kiss. She felt it when their lips touched, but more so when he kissed the top of her hand. Within a year and a half, he had graduated and she was well on her way. The wedding that proceeded his graduation was only natural.

They seemed to be the ideal couple. Her life was just as she imagined it. She was married to the epitome of chivalry, she had finished college and both of their careers were right on track. Life couldn't have been better. It could only get worse, and it did.

On one particular afternoon, Nadia decided to cook Brenden and herself a romantic meal. He needed one. They both needed one. She had some exciting news for him. She had made a decision that would change both of their lives forever. She was willing to give him the choice he wanted to make.

She made sure the corn was golden with butter, the carrots were a vibrant orange, the mashed potatoes were so fluffy the gravy collapsed their center, and a roast was cooked to perfection. She made sure she had just the right selection of music. Every item on the dinner table was symmetrical. The candles burned softly.

As time went on, the roast cooled. The corn was a soppy mess with an abundance of butter saturating the kernels. The carrots lost their shine.

The mashed potatoes were the color of mud from inhaling too much gravy for too long of a period of time. The playlist of music she had selected began to repeat. The items on the table were shifted due to her resting her head on the table. Finally, the candles had burned out. It was now midnight and Brenden had not returned home. Nadia was furious at the thoughts of what he must be doing. She thought he must be out with friends at a bar killing the brain cells that housed her initial decision.

"Perhaps the other guys were contaminating his brain with bad advice," she thought.

"He should be giving them advice. They are good for nothing. How could he turn to them for solutions for our issues instead of talking to me?"

An enraged Nadia immediately went to the kitchen and grabbed three large sized garbage bags. She went to their bedroom and began shoving all of his clothes into the bags.

"If he can make decisions about us without me, I'll make decisions without him. Let his asshole friends help him through this one."

Nadia grabbed one of the bags and headed toward the door. She flung open the door to toss the bag out but was startled by a man on the porch that was not Brenden. It was a police officer.

"Mrs. Scalloway?" the officer asked in an emotionless expression.

"Yes. I'm Mrs. Scalloway. What can I do for you officer?"

"Ma'am, I'm afraid that there has been an accident with your husband."

This only further angered Nadia.

"He goes out drinking with his friends and he is the one who must drive. They never seem to drive anywhere. Why does he let them walk all over him?" she thought to herself gritting her teeth.

"Where is he being held at? Was the car damaged at all?"

"Ma'am there were no cars involved. This was a different sort of accident. Your husband has been shot outside of a hospital on the west side of Lorain. We are not sure who is responsible. There was a group of protestors seen fleeing the scene but no one that could be identified."

Guilt rushed through Nadia's body. As she cursed his name at home, he was laying shot in a hospital. She wondered how she could doubt her husband, the man who never did her wrong in any way.

"What hospital is he at? How is he doing? Let me grab my coat so I can go see how he is."

"Ma'am, this is hard to say so I will just say it. Your husband was fatally wounded.

Nadia stopped where she was.

"Fatally?"

"Yes."

"Killed?"

"I'm afraid so, Ma'am."

Nadia turned around to face the police officer. He began giving her instructions on what to do and where to go. She shook her head in compliance with his instructions but her ears had fallen deaf. She thanked the officer as he stepped away from the porch. Nadia silently closed the door. She calmly walked over to the stereo and began to play the music once again. She then walked over to the dinner table and relit the candles. She sat down, served herself and began to eat the cold food.

She took a few bites of the roast and the side dishes and glanced over at the bag that she meant to toss out on the curb. She could feel her face increasingly heating up. Her hands and arms began to shake violently, and the food in her mouth fell out and back onto her plate. Her eyes hazed with tears as she thought of her husband shot dead. She yelled out as loud and she could as she stood up and threw the entire roast against the wall. She then picked up all of the dishes one by one and threw them against the wall. She flung her arms and cleared the table in one motion before she tipped over the entire table. She turned to her leather chair and began to beat it repeatedly until she had no energy left in her arms. She slowly sank to her knees and wrapped herself in the tablecloth and cried herself to sleep.

Nadia pressed Brenden to her as hard as she possibly could as she kissed his neck.

"I never thought I would be in your arms again," Nadia whispered to him.

"I always knew. I just had to be patient. I held on to patience like a winning lottery ticket. I kept it close to me never misplacing it. Now I have cashed it in."

Brenden intertwined his legs with hers as he put an arm around Nadia to stroke her hair.

"Did it hurt when you died?" Nadia asked him.

"I think I was too afraid to feel pain. All I could think of was that I was shot and I was dying. Everything lost its color, like watching a black and white television. The last thing I saw was the coward that shot me standing in front of me just as I fell. I tried to hold on, for you. I fought as long as I could but the reaper was too strong for me. How did you die?"

"I died in a plane crash."

"Who was your counselor when you arrived?" he asked.

"Peter," Nadia responded.

"Peter." They both said together as they shared a laugh.

"I was a mess. My clothes were filthy, my face was dirty and I was dead tired from his tour," Nadia explained.

"He definitely showed me everything there is here."

"Not nearly as much as you would think," Brenden quickly replied as he propped up his upper torso with his left elbow.

"Nadia, do you ever question some of the things you see here?"

"No, it is pretty much what I thought it would be."

"I see you have been here a while. Think of when you first arrived here. Wasn't there strange things happening?"

Nadia took a moment to concentrate.

"Yeah, there were a few things that confused me, but The Bible isn't exactly specific as to what Heaven is. Many of the descriptions are metaphoric descriptions."

Nadia propped herself up with her right elbow to face Brenden.

"What about this place has been bothering you?"

"The first thing is the lawless things I see."

"But Baby, that is why there are police here."

"Isn't heaven supposed to be sin free?" Brenden asked.

"I suppose, but men still control themselves," Nadia reasoned.

"How about all of these restricted areas? What is the explanation? We are not allowed to see our God? We are not allowed to see our savior Jesus Christ?

"I'm sure in due time. Things still have yet to play out. I bet it's for security reasons. I am sure they are extremely careful against terrorists from the other side."

"Ok, but what explains the missing people? My parents were devout Christians. Where are they? Where is Moses? Gandhi? How about Harriet Tubman? There are a lot of people that should be here that aren't. There are also people that I thought shouldn't be here that are."

"Brenden that just shows you that no one truly knows anyone. We never know what someone is like in their personal lives. Look outside. Look at this place. Is this not paradise?"

"I'm not sure about out there, but in here it sure does feel like it. There are questions in my head that bother me, but they don't mean as much now that I have what I want."

Brenden rolled her on top of him for a recap of the previous night.

That evening Nadia took a stroll to meet Beth at an outside café in Dundon. The sun was not close to setting, but its brilliance was losing its intensity. Nadia skipped along the boardwalk as the warm breezing floating off of the ocean twirled her around. Nadia waved to the children she met during her tour with Peter. The two Spanish girls along with the African boy smiled and waved. The Indian girl, however, simply waved with an emotionless expression on her face. Nadia arrived at the Café where she spotted Beth who was wildly waving her arms.

"Hey Woman, I'm over here," Beth shouted.

Nadia went over and joined Beth who had already ordered a tangerine margarita and a huge chicken club wrap.

"Beth that looks so good. Waiter, please bring me what she is eating and drinking."

"Beth stopped eating as soon as she looked into Nadia's face."

"Oh my, someone got some booty last night," Beth shouted.

"Shhh. Not so loud."

Both women stared at one another and began to laugh.

"Congratulations. You needed it. I bet Tyson missed you as much as you missed him."

"Tyson?"

Beth moved her entire plate to the far left of the table.

"You mean you didn't get ass from your husband?"

"Yes I did, it just wasn't Tyson," Nadia replied as she took a huge bite of her wrap.

"You have some explaining to do unless you were married to two men at once on Earth."

"Brenden Scalloway was my first husband. He was murdered when I was very young. I mourned for years, until I met Tyson. I fell in love with Tyson and we were married."

"What did Brenden have to say about Tyson?"

Nadia helped herself to another large bite of her wrap. Annoyed with the evasion, Beth pulled Nadia's plate away.

"You didn't tell Brenden about Tyson?"

"I didn't even think about it until you just brought it up," Nadia said defending herself before she grabbed her margarita and began taking large gulps through the straw.

"You may not have to. I mean, you haven't found Tyson after all this looking. He's got to be on the other side. This is Heaven, no situations like that could ever happen here. That's the perfect answer to everything. You were meant to spend your life with Brenden. Don't be ashamed of your love for him. Cherish it for eternity. So when are you getting some more lovin?" Beth asked giggling.

"I invited him over again tonight. I got some energy I must get released." Nadia answered laughing.

"Hey, I have some good news of my own. I haven't made any progress on getting Mary back but I have definitely made progress on my parents. I found out they are both here. I haven't found much on my mother, but I think I'm going to find out about my father very soon. From him I can find the rest of my answers.

"That's wonderful," Nadia said as she stood up to give her friend a hug.

"Things are starting to work out for the both of us, Nadia. Heaven is starting to feel like heaven."

"It just took a strong friendship to get us through all of this shit. Thank you for your friendship, Beth. I do not know what I would be doing right now if you hadn't saved me under that tree in the park."

"No thank you for being my friend, Nadia."

Both women stood there starting at each other hand in hand with tears of appreciation for one another.

Just over Beth's right shoulder, an event caught Nadia's eye. She spotted Peter sitting at a table alone with a newspaper pressed tightly to his face. Holding the newspaper as if it were a large steering wheel, he would slowly lower it just enough to expose his glasses and quickly raising it to cover his entire face. He wore a bright orange dress shirt with a green tie. The top two buttons were unfastened and the tie hung lazily low. His armpits were darkened from perspiration. Nadia had never seen Peter's appearance so unattended.

"Excuse me for a moment, Beth. I'm going to go over and see what this man is up to."

Nadia walked over to Peter's table and sat down. She immediately noticed the sweat that sprinkled his head.

"What in the world are you up to, Peter? Are you in some sort of danger?"

"No, I'm quite alright thanks for asking. I apologize if I am being rude, but today is a good day for me to appreciate my company on a solo basis."

"No, something is going on, and I'm not leaving until I find out."

Nadia scooted her chair next to Peter's until they were side by side. She raised her head and peaked over the newspaper to see what Peter was taking quick glimpses of. Across the patio, she spotted a woman in her forties with dark brown hair and blue eyes. She wore a long blue and white dress, with a matching large flower in her hair.

"You're sitting too close," Peter said in an annoyed state.

Peter proceeded to push Nadia's chair back over to where she initially was seated.

"I see what's going on. You see a woman that you want," Nadia said laughing.

"Please, I will see you tomorrow, Nadia. Have a good day."

"Why don't you just go over and talk to her?"

"Some things are best admired from afar."

"Peter, you don't have to be afraid. You have nothing to lose. If she goes out with you, then you get what you want. If she says no, then you are back where you started from. The worst thing that could happen is that you both become friends."

"Some things just aren't that easy, Nadia"

"You're right. Letting the woman of your dreams pass by is much easier," Nadia said as she stood up and walked back over to Beth.

"Hey Nadia, I must get going I have to get up bright and early tomorrow to track down my father."

"I better get going to, I have to get things ready for Brenden tonight," Nadia said with a grin.

Both women embraced and gave each other a simultaneous kiss on the cheek.

Nadia was off to her apartment to prepare to give Brenden a taste of his own medicine.

Chapter 13

Nadia decided to wear the same dress from their special night. It had kept the same red color as the night it ended in. She fixed her makeup the exact same way. She finished herself by putting her hair up exactly how it was. The entire apartment was illuminated by the soft light of candles. She cooked the identical dinner the night she lost him. The roast seemed slightly more tendeedr. The corn was slightly more golden. The carrots were a tad softer. The mashed potatoes were lighter than clouds. Nadia was even able to recreate her play list of music from that night. Everything seemed more perfect than it did that night. She thought that the night that was to be what was lost forever when the officer came to her door. It was not lost, only delayed. It was delayed for a better setting, in a better situation. That night was not meant to be had on Earth, but in Paradise.

Nadia heard the chimes ring throughout her apartment letting her know someone was downstairs waiting to be buzzed in. She pressed the button to activate the doors. She could taste her heart with her tongue. She quickly drank a glass of wine to ease her nerves. She then heard a knock on her apartment door. She activated the audio system and lit the fireplace. The fire seemed to be burn extremely large and bright this night.

"One moment, Honey."

She slowly walked over to the door. She clutched the long flat golden door handle but did not turn it. She took a deep breathe and closed her eyes. She reopened them upon exhale and turned the door handle to open the door.

The vision that filled Nadia's eyes made them increase two fold in diameter. She took a step back and would have stumbled backward if a strong hand had not caught her and pulled her close to him and kissed her.

"Tyson."

"Well it looks like Peter betrayed me and told you I was coming to surprise you tonight."

With his lanky arms he picked her up and she wrapped her legs around him so he would not drop her.

"Tyson…"

"Hush. Not a word from you."

"Tyson. I…"

"This is not a time for talking," Tyson said with a grin as he kissed her into silence.

He carried her to the bathroom and sat her on the sink. He never took his lips off of hers. He took both of his hands and ripped the bottom of her dress. As soon as the fabric was ripped, the dress lost its red hue and was returned to the original white color. Tyson placed his left hand on the small of Nadia's back and slowly lowered it lightly rubbing her backside. His hand found the knob to the faucet and turned it on.

"Remember this? We are right where we left off," Tyson whispered to her.

He then began to lightly splash the cool water against the warmth between Nadia's legs. The change in temperature sent a rush up Nadia's spine and throughout her body. Nadia thought she was going to

die from hypothermia. At that moment, Tyson
warmed her up with his warm breath. When his hot
tongue flickered in and out it caused an intense rush
again through Nadia's body once again. Tyson's licks
began to come at a faster rate, and deeper each minute.
Nadia felt her back relax and rest against the mirror.
The strain on her shoulders was at ease. She finally
rested her head back against the mirror in a trance as if
she was a drug addict feeling her fix. Her mouth was
slightly parted open as she let in deep breaths in and
out. Her eyes slowly filled with water until they
overflowed and dove out of her windows and perished
on her cheeks. Nadia could feel nothing but the region
where Tyson licked. She could not think of anything.
Everything failed to function. Her emotions had
reached their limit.

Tyson picked up Nadia once more. She tried to
wrap her soaked legs around him again, but she only
had the strength for one leg. He body limped over his
shoulder keeping her off the ground. He walked over
to the bedroom and laid her on the bed.
He hovered over her kissing her mouth and neck. She
could not blink. She just laid there emotionless.
Finally she looked over at him.

"Tyson?"

"Yes, Honey. It's me. It's alright. Everything is going to be alright now."

Tyson noticed Nadia was in a state of emotional shock.

"I know what you need. I'll make everything better. He removed himself from the bed and proceeded to blow out every candle in the apartment. Nadia heard the music in the apartment cease to play. Tyson then came back into the bedroom in complete darkness and silence.

Nadia heard a sound that was similar to a popping noise. She could feel Tyson kneeling over her. She then felt a cold smooth substance covering her shoulders and chest. It felt like syrup but slightly more fluid. It smelled sweet. Tyson then kissed her and proceeded down until he met the substance at her collar bones. He began to lick and eat the substance off her skin. He then began to eat it off of her full breasts. His pointed tongue slowly rubbing the substance across her nipples made Nadia's back arch with delight. He would cup her nipples with his lips that sent a light moan from her. He then lifted himself to place a long line of the substance down the middle of her breasts, down her stomach, and down to where it could go no farther. He began licking the center of her legs, drowning her clitoris with the substance. She began to let out long deep moans.

With a single lick, Tyson worked his tongue up the center of Nadia's stomach, between her breasts, up her neck and to her mouth. A rush of the substance flooded Nadia's mouth as she let it slide down her throat. She knew he had found the chocolate syrup in her refrigerator.

Tyson hovered himself over Nadia. The chocolate syrup worked as an adhesive and stuck their stomachs together. It also acted as a lubricant and Tyson entered Nadia with slow strokes. He quickly increased the pace as Nadia's heart rate increased. He was now at a rapid pace as Nadia thought her head would explode. He yelled in delight as she dug her nails into Tyson's back. This seemed to be the theme of the night. She doesn't remember the moment she passed out from exhaustion.

The next day, the sunshine staring in the window woke Nadia up. She looked over at Tyson who was clean and fast asleep. She assumed he woke up before she did, and took a shower. She got up and went to the shower to wash the sticky chocolate off of her body.

When she left the shower, she looked over at her answering machine. The message light was blinking the numeral one. She received a call from Brenden. He must have called while she was asleep. Tyson must have heard the message play in the morning. She felt cramping in her stomach. She could feel the blood rushing to her head. She slowly returned to the bedroom to face Tyson about Brenden. She should have confronted him last night, but her brain was not operational. She walked back into the bedroom to find Tyson awake staring at her with a blank stare. She crawled back into bed and sat next to him.

"Ok about the answering machine…"

"I know. I admit I turned down the sound when I woke up. The ringing gave me a headache. I'm sorry."

Nadia sighed in relief.

"You still have that habit I see. Just don't let it happen again."

"I promise," Tyson said as he learned over to give her a kiss.

"Last night you mentioned Peter. He was your counselor?

"Yeah, sneaky little weasel."

"Why didn't he tell me he knew where you were? He knew I was looking for you."

"Nadia, Peter has a huge case load. He probably didn't put two and two together. Do you know how many guys come here that look like me? Do you know how many Tysons come here? That doesn't matter anymore. What matters is I have found you and we can be together."

Tyson pulled Nadia closer to him.

"How did you find me?" Nadia asked.

"Very easily. If I would have thought of my idea in the beginning, we would have been together sooner. I knew you loved to teach. So I checked Escholar. It was very easy."

"Nadia, I have good news for you. Before you always mentioned that I was irresponsible at times. Well that has all changed here. I have a job that means something. I'm doing something that makes a difference. I'm in training for the police force. I am the cadet in charge. In time, I will be a full fledged Angel. Then I will be a part of the military that will fight against the other side when it is time to go to war."

Nadia sat up concerned.

"Tyson, I don't want you to get hurt."

"Don't worry Honey, our side will be victorious. We cannot lose. We have the big guy on our side. Do not worry."

Tyson sat up and began to put his clothes back on.

"I don't know how to explain this, but we cannot live together until my training is complete. It is forbidden for police officers until they are Angels."

He gave her a kiss on the forehead and left out the front door.

Nadia leaped to her feet, to check her answering machine.

"Hi, Nadia. This is Brenden. Listen, I'm sorry I wasn't able to make it last night. I've never let you down in the past other than that night and I won't start now. I will explain when I see you today. I need your help. Meet me in Heaven near the Main Building at 3:00pm. I will see you then."

Nadia checked her watch. It was 2:30pm. As quick as she could move, she dressed herself in jeans and a sweater and rushed out the door to meet him.

Chapter 14

Nadia and her driver arrived floating along the golden liquid in a gondola. The time was precisely 3:00pm. The light swaying created by the conduit in which they traveled put Nadia's body at ease. The ambiance of the ride temporarily erased the issues that plagued Nadia's conscious. She leaned back as the driver gracefully stroked the golden liquid with his ore. Her state of comfort was abruptly interrupted by a loud thud and shaking in the boat. Nadia quickly opened her eyes and sat up to see what the disturbance was.

"Brenden."

As quickly as he was identified by her, Brenden rushed over to her and began kissing her as he moved her body to his. As he pushed her on top of him it became apparent to Nadia that the intent of the kiss was to mask his presence from those who may be watching instead of showing affection.

They lightly glided along fully embraced. Brenden kept one eye exposed waiting until there was an opening. As soon as there was a moment void of anyone's attention, Brenden quickly stood to his feet pulling Nadia up at the same time. They hopped off of the golden gondola at the next staircase.

"Hey, what about my money?" the driver yelled as he continued to float without them.

Brenden took the lead walking up the stairs that led to the sidewalk level. He peered over the last step to see if anyone was in the immediate vicinity. He looked with caution, but with confidence that no one would detect him easily with every object in the city being under the same vale of a golden hue. When he looked around he noticed a few patrolmen surveying the area. Brenden quickly lowered his head.

"Shit."

This was the first time Nadia ever heard Brenden curse. This is the first time she had seen his behavior so erratic.

Once again Brenden slowly raised his line of sight over the top stair. He saw that the patrolmen had moved on to another area. He quickly grabbed Nadia's hand and nearly pulled her up the flight of stairs with him. As soon as they were both on sidewalk level, Brenden ushered Nadia over to a small area that was crowded with trees. They both kneeled behind opposing trees staring at one another panting.

"What is going on, Brenden? Why are we doing this?"

"I will explain later. There is no time right now, Honey. We just have to get away from this place for the time being," Brenden said still out of breath.

After a moment Brenden leaped to his feet with his back still tightly pressed against the golden bark of the tree. Nadia mimicked his motions as they were both upright and peeking around the trees. As quiet as he could, Brenden grabbed Nadia's hand and began leading her through a maze of bushes. They both were prodded by loose branches from the bushes. Brenden paid no mind in his haste, yet Nadia was growing more irritated with each twig.

The both of them finally came to a clearing. The two of them stood atop of a hill that led down to a

fenced piece of land. Once again Brenden took Nadia
by the hand and lowered her to her backside along with
him. He began sliding down the hill bringing her
along for the ride. Finally they both made it to the
bottom of the hill and walked gingerly near the
wooded golden fence.

Nadia looked through the fence and saw some
of the most beautiful animals her eyes had ever taken
in. The field was full of giant golden doves. The
doves were the size of the minivan her and Brenden
owned on Earth.

"Oh my God, Brenden they are so beau..."

Nadia cut herself short as she saw Brenden
kicking a hole in the bottom of the wooded golden
fence.

"Brenden, have you lost your mind? You are
begging to go to jail or worse yet banished to the other
side."

"Nadia shut up. Please," Brenden urgently said
talking through his teeth.

"We are almost away from here."

Nadia was once again taken aback by the total
personality change by Brenden. He was always calm
and reserved. He always was sensible in his actions

and everything he did had a logical reason. She did not recognize this erratic, mysterious, semi-sane man she was once married to.

Brenden accomplished kicking an opening at the bottom of the fence and they both crawled through. Keeping a low base, the two of them quickly walked over to one of the large doves.

"Shhh. Hey now big mamma," Brenden whispered to the bird as he caressed its feathers.

Brenden then took a knife from his sock and began to cut the rope that held the bird to the ground.

"C'mon Nadia, up you go."

Nadia reluctantly placed her foot in Brenden's hands as he raised her up to the top of the Dove. He then took a giant leap to give himself a head start. He too was on the Dove.

"Yeah! Yeah!" Brenden shouted with a kick to the bird's sides.

The dove exposed its large golden wings. The bird began to steadily beat them as they began to lift off the ground. Once they were a few meters off the ground, the bird's ascension began to increase.

"Halt. Stop."

Nadia and Brenden both looked down to find that there were seven officers staring up at them. She could not tell if any of them were Tyson. She hoped if she could not identify the officers, they could not identify her. The officers began to open fire on the dove but their aim was not nearly close enough. They were too far away to be an accurate target. A fear suddenly had taken her over. She wondered if they would begin to fly up to them. They would be sent to the other side for sure. She then remembered Tyson explaining to her that only military personnel have the ability to fly with wings. Officers in training had not earned that ability. They were safe.

Brenden guided the dove up and over the clouds. As they continued to climb, the golden hue slowly faded away from them, and the natural color of things began to fade in. The giant white dove was now gliding high over the clouds.

"Brenden, where are we going?"

"I'm taking you to a place I wanted to take you last night, but didn't have the opportunity to. It may not be as romantic being that we are fashionably a mess right now."

Nadia noticed that the dove began to steadily climb. The air increasingly became thin.

"Do you think we have flown high enough? I don't think they are going to catch us now," Nadia said as she tried to speak over the wind.

"Oh I'm not concerned with them. We've lost them. This is the way we are supposed to go."

As the ride continued, Nadia's heart rate began to decrease to a normal rate. She was in disbelief of the fact that Brenden was the cause of such suspense. This was the man who did not J-Walk. She had just witnessed him eluding the authorities and commit theft. On Earth she urged him to be slightly more adventurous but never meant to this degree. After feeling a bit more comfortable, she leaned into his back and rested her head in between his shoulder blades. She squeezed his waist tightly and took in a deep breath.

The comfort was short lived as the dove sharply began an incline once again. The speed began to intensify as the incline increased. Nadia was now holding on to Brenden as tightly as she could so she would not fall from the dove. The higher they went the warmer the temperature became. Nadia was certain they would burn up on the bird, but just as she could no longer take the heat, comfort was upon her once more.

The bird floated in the dark space. Nadia expected to see a planet beneath them from which they left but there was none. There were only the tiny spots of stars that surrounded them. There was no trace of the three suns that illuminated Heaven anywhere.

In the far distance, Nadia could spot a star that appeared slightly more illuminated than its surrounding neighbors. The silver sphere grew larger and brighter the closer they got to it. After a few moments the object was clearly visible. They were approaching a small moon that appeared to be a pearl that rested peacefully in the center of the abyss.

The dove landed gracefully on the dusty surface. Brenden dismounted first, and then helped Nadia off of the bird. As soon as they were off, the dove laid on the surface and began to rest.

Brenden gently grabbed Nadia's hand and proceeded to lead her over to a small table with a single silver candle. There were two places that were set. Brenden pulled out one of the chairs and gestured for Nadia to take a seat. With a gentle smile, Nadia sat in the seat and Brenden eased her to the table. He then sat himself opposite of her at the table.

The both of them had shining silver trays in front of them. Nadia took her lid off and was astonished to find out that she had a plate full of golden corn, vibrant orange carrots, fluffy white mashed potatoes smothered in gravy and the main tenant on her plate was a slice of tender roast.

"How did you know this was the meal?" Nadia said with a gasp.

"Know what, Honey?"

"This is the meal. This is meal that I was going to cook you that night."

"It was prepared with love. Perhaps this is why this is the meal. You had cooked this meal for me? I didn't think with our circumstance at the time you would want to cook anything for me. What was so special about that night?"

Nadia thought back about that night and the revelation she was going to present to Brenden. She did not want to go back to that night. Not only because of the thought of losing Brenden, but it was no longer necessary to tell him of her thoughts at that moment in time.

"Forget about that meal and that night. This meal looks so much better. This night is so much clearer."

"And you, my wife, are just as beautiful."

Nadia could not help but to blush.

"Hey Mister, your sweet words won't make me forget about what just happened. What was all of that?"

Without lifting his head from his plate, Brenden lightly put down his eating utensils. When he finally did look up at Nadia, he had a business like expression to him.

"The day I was supposed to come over, I went to Heaven to make arrangements for the next morning. This is where I wanted to take you. I visited the farm where we picked this dove from to schedule it for today. After being unsuccessful in being approved for one, I went to find answers why I couldn't rent one. I walked past the Main Building when I spotted something out of the corner of my eye. It was a dark shadowy figure lurking in the side alley of the Main Building. He was completely dark as if he were covered in tar. He was tall with a slight muscular build. He had long curly hair that reached his shoulders. Everything about him was black. His hair, skin and clothes were all pitch black. Even the wings on his back resembled those of a crow. The only things that weren't black on him were his eyes. The whites of his eyes contrasted brilliantly against his dark complexion. His eye color was not to be forgotten. They were a burning orange. It was as if I was looking at a dark angel from the other side.

He was moving about in the alley when I saw him enter an open door. My curiosity got the best of me. I knew it was forbidden, but if he was from the other side I had to find out what he was up to. I entered the door and I found myself in a corridor. I silently walked around from corridor to corridor with no sign of him. Every once in a while, I would hear voices coming toward me and I would duck in a room.

During one instance when I had to duck into a room, I found an information center. It was an enormous room that had computers everywhere. I sat down at one of the terminals and noticed it was a database full of names. This one was different from the ones in Escholar. It had more information in detail on everyone. Just as I found in Escholar, there were some names that should have been here and names that should not have been here. I began digging more and more into the records trying to piece things together when I saw a shadow move by the door. I stopped what I was doing and went in the direction I thought the shadow went.

I went down a few corridors when two Angels were coming towards me. I did not want to get caught in an area I was not supposed to be in so I ducked inside another door. The door led to a platform that was maybe one hundred meters above a room. It was a room that was as big as a football stadium. Below me were a series of metal landings that circled the room similar to the one I was standing on. The room was filled with many Angels in exercise trainings ranging from hand to hand combat, to weapons training. The physical things these angels were able to perform were something that I could not believe. Their strength and speed were far superior to any athlete Earth had ever seen. The weapons were not fired, but you saw what their pistols looked like. I can only imagine what the larger artillery would do.

Two platforms above the surface where the training was taking place were two men walking along their platform that traveled the diameter of the room. One man was tall and muscular. He had long curly hair and a medium length beard. He had brown eyes. He wore white shoes, white slacks, and a white dress shirt. His top two buttons were undone. Attached to his side, was a sword encased in a sheath. There was a man that was much shorter that walked along with him. He wore a white cloak that completely engulfed him except for his mouth and long nose. His white wrinkled hands barely stuck out of his long sleeves. His left hand held a white cane that helped his frail body keep up with the vigorous steps of the taller, younger gentleman.

The older man was explaining to the younger gentleman about what was taking place. He told them that they were almost ready for their preemptive strike. The other side had seriously underestimated their power. They have an army in the zillions. They severely outnumber the other side. The other side is no match. Upon hearing this, the younger gentleman expressed his pleasure. He stated that his father would be very pleased. He said that soon they would crush the other side. Soon they would rule the Earth. The older gentleman chimed in and told him they could rule the other side as well as Earth.

Then suddenly there was loud noise that came from the other side of my landing. The shadowy figure had dropped his camera. The younger gentleman looked up to see what the noise was. The shadowy figure took off in one direction and I went in the other. I frantically rushed through the corridors trying to find my way out. I came to one corridor where there were two Angels talking to one another. I could hear footsteps coming behind me. Before I was caught, I slipped once again into a side room. I could hear the angels that were behind me ask the two angels in the corridor if anyone had come this way. The angels had not seen me so they replied no. I heard them run down the corridor, but I could hear the other two still in the corridor.

I was stuck in the room.

I knew I could not leave and risk being caught. I looked around for any means of escape. I found a small duct on one of the walls. I removed the cover and maneuvered my way through it. I found that it led to an opening, but an opening that had a combination of people and officers standing around. I knew I could escape but not on foot. It was too big of a risk of being caught. I returned to the room and gave you a call that

night to pick me up at 3:00am. When I saw you I
made my run for it."

Nadia was shocked at the story Brenden told to
her. It was so out of his character.

"The younger, man must have been Jesus,"
Nadia said.

"No. At first I thought perhaps it was Jesus
also but he could not have been. This man had a
sinister look to him. When he talked about ruling
Earth and war it pleased him. That is something that
disturbs me. Why is our side holding a preemptive
strike? Why would our side want to rule Hell?"

"I guess it is something we will find out."

"You're right. And much sooner than later.
Whatever is going to happen, will happen soon. From
what I heard they are ready."

Brenden felt that their romantic evening was
turning into a military debate. He stood up and took
Nadia's hands and lifted her to her feet.

"Like you said, tonight's meal has been so
good. Tonight seems so much clearer. Let's forget
about war, and make love."

Brenden pulled Nadia, close and gave her a soft, slow kiss. He lowered his hands behind her and began to lightly kiss her neck.

Nadia had many things to think about. She thought about Brenden's story and a possible war with the other side. There was a separate war that was waging in her heart. A civil war was taking place and the combatants were Tyson and Brenden. She managed not to think about it until Brenden began to touch her. She was too exhausted to witness a battle at the time. She pulled herself away from Brenden for the moment.

"What's wrong Nadia? This is our chance not only to make love to the moon, but on the moon."

"I'm just tired, Honey." Nadia replied.

She was half right. She had very little sleep over the past few days. She was mentally and physically drained.

"Please take me home."

"Ok, it is not a problem Sweetheart."

The two climbed on the dove and began their decent back.

Chapter 15

Nadia was extremely exhausted the next day. The few days began to wear on her. Her eyes sported bags underneath them. Her skin was usually pale, but now it was also flush. Her hair also did not have the red shine it normally did. Her body was running on empty.

No matter the level of exhaustion, Nadia was prepared and energized for class. Ever since she arrived, teaching was her escape from her personal problems. This particular night she stayed late to do more preparation and grading. She also talked with Rodney by phone.

"Rodney, I am impressed that you have been holding a low B average. That is much better than what you had with me at Elyria State. Your behavior is quite the same. You miss my classes, you turn in your homework late, and you sleep in my class when you are there. Rodney, I thought you had turned a new leaf. I thought you and I were finally cool."

"Mrs. McKline it is not what you think. I have been working my ass off trying to keep that B average. I really do put as much effort into your class as you want me to but it is just hard. My tuition is crazy right now. I am working three jobs to keep up. If I don't work, I don't get the scholarship money the school is giving me now. I'm dog tired when I do your homework but I still do it. When I miss your class, I'm not missing because I'm being irresponsible, but because I'm at work. I sleep in your class at times because that is the only time I have to sleep. I only sleep during the times when you are going over assignments and review. I'm sorry Mrs. McKline, but I'm doing what I got to do."

Nadia could hear the strain in Rodney's voice over the phone.

"Rodney, you sound miserable. Why don't you just take a semester off and sort things out."

"That would violate my scholarship. If I do that I would be kicked out of school. They didn't tell me this, but I think if I get kicked out of school, I may be sent to the other side."

"Rodney that is crazy."

"I know, but that's the vibe I get. I ain't going to try these people."

"Well just hang in there Rodney. Remember where you are. It will all work out."

"You too Mrs. McKline. You have been looking a lot like I do lately. Goodbye."

Nadia flipped her phone shut. She took her compact out of her purse and attempted to apply makeup to her tired face. No matter how much makeup she applied to the bags underneath her eyes, they were still bags. In frustration, she walked toward the front door.

She saw where storm clouds covered the sky waiting to burst. She also saw flashes of intense lightning leaping from one cloud to the next putting on a dazzling display of power. As she approached the door she saw the rain pouring down violently striking everything outside in large liquid drops. Nadia grew accustomed to the fact that people did not get wet during rainstorms. When she stepped outside she was shocked to find herself being drenched in the downpour. She did not have an umbrella because she did not own one. She did not own one because there was never any need for one. She stepped outside to see if she could catch a cab home. Normally she walked to work. To her surprise, there were no cabs to be hailed. There wasn't anyone. There were no students shuffling to class. There were no officers patrolling the streets. There were no vendors on the sidewalks selling food. She was completely alone on a deserted campus. She stepped out on the street to see what was going on. The thunder began to grow louder with each strike. The flashing lightning was her only opportunity to see around her since the streetlights were out.

On one particular flash, Nadia was able to make out a dark silhouette of a man with an umbrella standing at the opposite end of the street. When the flash went away, she could no longer see him until the next. She wondered if this was the shadowy figure that Brenden had told her of. Whoever it was they faced her and they were the only two on the street. Her first instincts told her to run as fast as she could in the opposite direction, but there was nowhere to run. The way Brenden described the speed of this thing; it would certainly catch her before she left the street. Her only choice was to walk toward the figure and see what its intentions were.

As the distance between her and the figure, along with the intervals between lightening flashes decreased, she could see it was not a shadowy figure but a familiar one. It was Peter. He stood there with a blank stare on his face. He was dressed in a suit. Despite his umbrella, Peter was being pelted by the large and fast raindrops. It was as if he was not holding an umbrella at all. The glasses on his face were completely fogged.

"Peter, what in the world is…"

"This is Paradise Nadia," Peter said with a stern voice.

"In paradise, everyone is supposed to be content. Everyone is supposed to be happy. Everyone's needs are met. There is no hunger. There is no cold. There is no homelessness. Everything is the way it should be here yet it appears that some people cannot be satisfied with that. I don't know what happens on Earth that makes people not have the ability to be thankful for what they have. People have to have answers. People have to know why. People have to wonder if what they have is what they should have. People even question if Paradise is good enough for them.

Peter took off his glasses to wipe them. He did not put them back on.

"Nadia, your actions do not go unnoticed here. No one's actions go unnoticed. Your actions have been discomforting to many people who make decisions here. I do not represent them now, I am here as your friend. Please Nadia, do not question paradise. Do not question perfection. Enjoy it. You are meant to enjoy everything here for your deeds on Earth. Many people from Earth use the saying the grass is greener on the other side. The other side has no grass Nadia. Do not wish to see it for yourself."

There was a long period between lightning flashes. Once another one came, Nadia noticed that Peter was gone. She was once again alone in the middle of the dark street. For the first time since arriving, she felt in danger. She hurried home as quickly as she could.

When Nadia returned to her apartment she found that all of her lights were on. She immediately dropped her briefcase and removed her soaked coat and placed it on the floor. She quietly stepped into the living room area. She glanced over at the bar and saw where a glass had been used and bottles had been opened. She walked into the living room area.

"Hello? Who is here?" she yelled.

She could hear a noise coming from the bedroom. She slowly picked up a poker from the fireplace and slowly walked towards the bedroom. She tried to use as much stealth as she could muster but she thought that whoever was in her bedroom would certainly hear her heartbeat approaching.

When she finally reached the slightly opened bedroom door, she stopped. She slowly clutched the handle and took a deep breath. She flung the door open and immediately let go of the poker.

It was Brenden.

"Brenden, how did you get in? What are you doing?"

Brenden still had his trench coat on with a black sweater and black slacks on underneath. He was soaked from head to toe. His hair was a mess. He kept his head lowered to a sheet of paper in his hands. Even though his head was lowered, Nadia could tell he still had not shaven since his ordeal in the city of Heaven. He began to read a note.

"My Dear loving wife,
I am so happy to have you in my life. It has felt like eternity since we were together. I hate not living together but I hope soon that can change. I look forward to running my fingers through your long, thick hair again. I look forward to the day we can make love every night. I miss you so much, Sweetheart. This will truly be Paradise for me, when you and I are one once more."

"Brenden. Sweetheart, that is so sweet of you. It has really made my day. I was having one…"

"Love, Tyson," Brenden said softly.

Nadia took a gasp and stumbled backwards as her eyes filled with tears.

"Brenden…"

"I thought we were soul mates. I thought we had a bond, Nadia. I thought when we said we would be together it was to be forever."

Brenden picked up his head and exposed his bloodshot eyes. He also had heavy bags underneath them. Nadia could see veins on his temples bulging with intensity. His hands clutched the paper that contained the words tightly to where his knuckles were white.

"How could you do this to me? Do you realize that I waited here all these years for you? My dreams of us being here together as a family are just fucked now."

"Tyson, did you expect me to be a lonely woman forever? Did you really expect me to just spend the rest of my life lonely?" Nadia said in her defense.

"I expected my wife to wait for me!" Brenden screamed as he stood up.
"I expected my wife to love me as I loved her. What did you expect would happen when you got here? Did you ever think of me? Did you ever visit my grave or did you just act as if I never existed?"

"Brenden, please stop. You're drunk. Let's talk about this."

"There is nothing to talk about!" Brenden yelled striking the wall next to Nadia's head

The instance he struck the wall the entire wall shook causing the painting on the wall to fall down and the items on the dresser next to Nadia to come crashing on the floor. The tears that filled Nadia's eyes ran down her face in sorrow and fear. Her eyes lowered to the poker near the door. Brenden noticed.

"Oh I see. That is how you want to talk about this. That is your idea of fixing this."

"Please, Baby I would never hurt you."

"Oh yeah? What do you call this situation?" Brenden shouted.

"I love you!" Nadia shouted at the top of her lungs.

"You love yourself!" Brenden screamed back.

"You love your little fantasy of having two husbands. Did you ever realize that adultery is a sin?" Paradise? This is now Hell for me. You have condemned me to Hell! If you love me when I turn to walk out that door you will drive that poker through my back."

Brenden stormed out of the bedroom door. Nadia could hear him knocking things over in the living room before slamming the door shut.

Nadia sunk to her knees in her soaked clothes. She sat there and cried. She cried as loud as she wanted to. She did not care for the consideration of her neighbors. She did not want to be the only person in Paradise suffering. She needed someone to understand her suffering and pain. She needed someone to be there for her.

There was one person who could.

There was one person who would.

Chapter 16

Nadia arrived at Beth's house by foot as quickly as she could. She hoped that Beth would not be terribly upset at the timing of her visit, but the fact that she was coming at such a late hour would be a clear indication of the dire mood that had taken hold of her. The warm night air had somewhat dried Nadia's clothes to where they were only damp. Her thick red hair was very damp and matted from absorbing the rain earlier that night.

Nadia walked up to the door to find it wide open and hanging in the frame by a single hinge. Nadia rushed in with fear taking a seat next to the sorrow that was in her heart.

"Beth? Beth where are you?" Nadia screamed out.

Inside the living room she found a room that was decimated. The glass coffee table was smashed with its contents spilled on the ground. The vase that once rested in the center of the coffee table was shattered with the liquid inside spilled all over the golden carpet. The fireplace held a collection of DVD movies and CD's. They were all blackened with soot that was also spilled out in the immediate vicinity of the fireplace. The love seat was overturned with the contents that stuffed it spilled out.

The sight of the scrambled room did not frighten Nadia as much as the six men that she saw standing in the room. They were all much taller than ordinary men. They all were dressed in all black robes that came down to their knees with black belts around their waists. They wore black combat boots with handles of a single dagger in each boot. Each was armed with a sheathed black sword at their sides with a semi-automatic firearm strapped to their backs. Each had variations of hair styles. Some had small afro-style haircuts. A couple had military style short haircuts. The leader seemed to have long curly hair that was similar to Tyson's.

Those were not the most frightening features to Nadia. Each man had long feathery wings that were tucked neatly at their backs. The feathers were slick and black like that of a raven's. Their skin was black as space and slick as oil. It was if they were made of tar. The most glaring feature was their intense orange eyes that contrasted brilliantly against their dark skin.

Their description was exactly how Brenden described the shadowy figure. She knew where they were from and she knew why they were in Beth's home.

"What did you do with my friend?" Nadia shouted at the men.

"This issue is for parties involved only, Ma'am. If you are not family or directly involved in this matter, then you must leave," the leader said.

He was slightly taller than the others and definitively more vocal.

"Who are you to tell me what I can and cannot do? If I want to speak with my friend, that's what I will do!"

Nadia went to strike the leader but before her fist could reach the halfway point of its destination, he had taken hold of wrist. Her second attempt with her left fist resulted in the same conclusion. Her wrists immediately began to burn from being in contact with his dark, slick skin. Before his hands burned through her wrists, the leader threw Nadia to the ground.

"If you don't want any trouble Ma'am I suggest you move along."

Nadia laid there in the water that saturated the carpet. Tears rolled down her eyes as she looked back up at the leader. She was slowly losing everything and everyone dear to her. She was not going to lose her friend. Without Beth, she was sure to go insane.

While on the ground, she reached for a sharp portion of the broken glass table. She clutched it so tightly, that she cut her own hand without her knowledge. At this moment she did not know pain. She would not let pain stop her from saving Beth from the other side.

As she stood up to lunge at the leader, she saw one of his associates walked over to him and began whispering in his ear. He then flashed his finger in Nadia's direction. As the both of them looked in her direction, she quickly dropped the shattered glass from the table and sunk back down. The leader walked back over to her.

"Are you Nadia?" he asked.

Nadia did not know how to reply. She wondered if perhaps she was somehow implicated in Beth's situation. She wondered if they thought she and Beth were lovers. She did not want to go to the other side, but at the same time she had to hold on to the last thing she had left and that was her principle. She no longer had anything to lose. She didn't handle her situation with Tyson and Brenden the way she should have, but she was determined to be an honorable friend until the end even if it meant eternity in Hell. Nadia stood up, brushed the water and debris from her clothes while straightening them out. She wiped the tears from her face and raised her chin.

"Yes, I am Nadia," she said confidently awaiting any consequence that would befall her.

"It would have been easier if you said that from the start. You may talk to Beth."

Nadia walked into the bedroom, to find Beth quietly sitting on the bed. Four more of the men were in the room with her.

Beth's face was completely red. Her eyes were puffy from constant crying. She held an unopened black book in her hand as she sat there.

"Beth? Hello? Hi, it's me, Nadia."

Beth just sat there with the same expressionless face.

"Men, let's give these two a moment," said the leader.

The men then left the room closing the door behind them both. Nadia sat to the right of Beth on the bed and placed her left arm around her to console her.

"Honey talk to me."

Beth raised heavy head to look at Nadia.

"Nadia? Nadia," Beth whispered as she broke down crying and buried her face in Nadia's shoulder.

Nadia joined her in her sorrow as she embraced Beth. They both sobbed as hard as they could for ten minutes until they could cry no longer. Beth raised her head and wiped the tears from her eyes. Nadia kept her hands tightly intertwined with Beth's.

"Sorry about the snot," Beth said as both women had a slight laugh.

"Beth, I don't know what to say. I don't want you to go. I'll do anything I can to bring you back here."

"Don't. You will just find yourself in the same situation I am in now. There is no use for that."

Beth freed her hands from Nadia's and used them to raise her head by her chin.

"Hey. There is a good thing about all of this. All of my time being here, in this perfect place, eating this delicious food, filling my lungs with this clear air, I was not truly happy. My soul was in Heaven, but my spirit was with her in Hell. I was silently being tortured without her. My true suffering will come to an end.

"I still don't think you deserve Hell, Beth. You have a great soul. You have been there for me so many times since I have been here."

Nadia could barely control her emotions.

"I don't know what I would have done if it were not for you. I love you Beth. You are the best friend anyone could ever ask for. Even though you are there, you will always be an angel to me. I swear you don't deserve Hell."

"Hell?" Beth asking mockingly.

"Would it truly be that for me? I may burn. They may rip flesh of my bones. I may be tortured and beaten. But I will be with Mary. We will be together forever. No matter what happens, I will be with the one thing I've always wanted. Love is worth enduring anything. No, I won't be in Hell. I won't be here, but I will be happier than I've ever been."

Both women embraced once more.

"It's so bittersweet."

"You seem like you're totally OK with going. What is bittersweet?"

"Finally finding my parents and having to say goodbye. That's the bittersweet part."

Nadia pulled Beth away at arms' length in shock.

"You have found your parents?"

"Yep."

"Who are they? Have you talked to them? What are they like?" Maybe I can give them a last message."

"I am sure you can give them a last message for me. To my father at least. I have talked with my mom, but not my father. It turns out they were from Earth. My father died first. He was murdered while my mom was pregnant. When my mom recovered from the shock of losing my father, she aborted me. I was then born here where I grew up in an orphanage. My mother arrived not too long ago."

Nadia closed her eyes and let her mind leap back in time. She jumped back to the night she and Brenden were to have dinner. She could see the cold roast sitting on the table. She could see the cold corn and the mashed potatoes drowned in the cold gravy. She saw herself sitting there staring at the extinguished candles. She remembered thinking of the thoughts that were going through her mind. She was thinking of the nervousness. She was angry with Brenden for not coming home, because of the anxiety she held in her stomach. That night was the night she was to tell him that she had decided to keep the baby. It was something he wanted but she did not. He wanted a little girl more than anything in the world. They had argued about this for an entire week. She felt that a child at the moment would hinder both of their careers. She had prepared the dinner as a peace offering. He had convinced her that they could make it work. That night, they were to become a family. That night they would get back to love. Nadia then saw the policeman come to the door. She could not hear his words, but she could remember them perfectly. She then saw herself fall back in tears.

Nadia's eyes opened once more and saw Beth looking back at her with the same eyes.

"That is why they let me back here," Nadia whispered.

"Because we are family," Beth whispered back.

Nadia took a moment. She was no longer looking at the friend she knew since she had arrived, but the daughter she had never known. They both hugged for the last time, and cried for the last time.

"Baby I'm so sorry. I love you. I'm so sorry," Nadia cried in Beth's shoulder.

"It's alright, Mother. I love you also. I always have. I will take your love with me and I want you to keep mine so we will never be apart again."

The door opened and the troops were standing at the door. Darkness filled the doorway where the troops stood. It was a gateway to the other side.

"It is time," the leader told the women.

Nadia tried to clutch on to Beth's arm, but Beth stood up regardless. Nadia stood up and gave her daughter one last hug. Beth did not want to delay what was to happen and pulled herself away. Before she stepped through the gateway with the shadowy figures, Beth turned around once more.

"Fix your situation before it's too late. Love cannot be tricked or delayed. Endure what you must, but make peace with love. Love is worth more than anything else here. Love is worth going to Hell for."

"I love you Beth."

"I love you Mom."

Nadia stepped into the doorway and the darkness consumed her. Each of the dark figures stepped into the doorway with the dark consuming them also. The last thing Nadia saw was their orange eyes slowly dissipate. Finally the leader stepped through and closed the door.

In a last attempt to save her daughter, Nadia ran to the bedroom door to get her back. When she opened the door she stumbled on debris left in the hallway and fell into the living room area. In the moment that she found her aborted daughter, she was gone once again.

The only thing Nadia could do was cry herself to sleep. The living room was appropriately left in a chaotic state. Nadia felt at home in the mess. A mess that was symbolic to her situation.

Chapter 17

The next morning, Nadia found herself packaged in her own comforter on her own bed. She must have walked home at some point the previous night. The constant ringing of her telephone was what woke her. She had listened to the previous messages without any intentions of falling out of bed to answer them.

"Nadia this is Helena. Where are you? I have students reporting you AWOL. You have not called off. That is normally grounds for termination but you're the best professor we have. You better call me very soon or else."

"Yo Professor McKline its Rodney. I need you to correct my grade on the project for the midterm like you said you would. If you don't change it by next week it will be too late and I'll have a C average. If I don't keep it at a B, I don't know what will happen but I'm sure you and I can guess."

None of these dire issues could force Nadia to leave the solitude she found in bed. Her blankets were a barrier that protected her from any harm that was yet to come. The next message convinced her to get out of bed.

"Hey Nadia it's me Tyson. I miss you, Honey. I can't go another day without seeing you. Meet me at Milner's as soon as you can"

Nadia instantly felt her stomach warm with hope. Perhaps this was how things were to end. Before that moment, she thought that she had lost a daughter. She now believed that she had found her aborted daughter she never knew. She was thankful for the opportunity to know her only child so well. She also thought perhaps her situation with both of her husbands may have worked itself out. Brenden reacted to the situation by running away. She knew she had to tell Tyson about Brenden. She was not sure how he would react but in her heart she knew that he would handle the news much easier than Brenden. She wondered if it was a blessing in disguise. The last she saw of Brenden she was in fear. His behavior had deteriorated ever since she was reunited with him. She did find his newfound edginess invigorating but not at the expense of sanity. He just could not accept the notion of paradise. In contrast, Tyson had become everything she wanted him to be. He now had the sense of responsibility and purpose. The more she thought about Tyson, the more she was able to convince herself that he was the one she was meant to be with. She even began to believe that it was fate that Brenden was killed because he was not the one to make her happy. It was Tyson.

Nadia arrived at Milner's as fast as she could. She had showered away the dirt and tears that filled her skin. She was beautiful once again. She looked around but did not see Tyson immediately. She sat at the bar to wait for him.

"Hey Beautiful Red," Milner said playfully.

"Well hey there, Sir. Can you get me one of those special hot chocolates with something special in it?"

"You bet. Hey you seem to be a little livelier today. Did you drop a hot coal in your britches?"

"No. I am just learning to enjoy what I have here and what is around me. I am learning to be like you."

"My condolences," Milner said with a wink.

"What is that supposed to mean?"

"It means that my artificial smile is for my customers. You do not have any customers so I am assuming your artificial smile is due to a lack of sanity."

"Are you saying that you are not happy? Look, you have your own bar and grille. It's full of customers all of the time. You are living your dream here."

"Yes that's true but this dream comes with a hefty price. See anyone else working here? It's because I can't afford to hire help. This place is packed wall to wall with people every day and I have to wait on them all hand and foot. I cook the food, serve the drinks and clean the dishes. I am security and the janitor and the handyman. I can't close for a day or take a vacation because I need every dollar I get to invest back into this place. I can't raise prices. People can barely afford to come here as it is. I can't sell the business or just quit because of the enormous loan I received to open. A loan that the interest grows by leaps and bounds. I honestly feel stuck. But it's my dream right?"

Nadia lowered her head as Milner served her a drink. She turned around and saw Peter sitting alone at a table. She decided to walk over and join him.

"Hey Peter. I just want to apologize for anything that I may have done to jeopardize my situation here. I won't be associating myself with anyone..."

"Yeah that's great Nadia," Peter said without even looking in Nadia's direction.

"Right now I must go do something that I should have done long ago."

"What's that?"

"Take your advice."

Peter stood up and adjusted his shoulders while putting on his sport coat. He then proceeded to walk over to a woman that he saw sitting at the bar. Nadia realized it was the same woman he had his eye on when she met Beth for lunch. She could not decipher what he was saying but she could tell he was speaking confidently. The woman flashed him a bright smile as they shook hands. She could tell as Peter continued to talk the more he relaxed.

Suddenly a large man in a white tank top with his hair in corn rows approached Peter and the woman. Nadia could tell that the man was angry with Peter for approaching his girlfriend. Before Peter could apologize, the man had thrown a drink that sat on the bar in Peter's face and threw him to the floor. Everyone sitting at the bar, including the woman began to laugh at Peter as he struggled up to his feet. Red with embarrassment, Peter began to storm out. Nadia intercepted him at the door.

"Peter."

"I guess love isn't for everyone after all," Peter said hastily as he pushed his way past her and out of the door.

"What was his problem?"

Nadia turned around to see who was talking to her.

"Tyson," Nadia said as she gave him a big hug and kiss.

"We have to sit down. There is something we have to talk about."

Nadia led Tyson to an empty table and they both sat down. Nadia made sure never to let go of Tyson's hands. The confidence that she held this morning had not transformed into nervousness.

"Tyson, I won't sugarcoat this. This may be painful, but if we are going to be together, I have to tell you this. I hope that we can put this past us and move forward."

"Hey it's alright. Just come out with it."

Nadia closed her eyes and took a long breath.

"Tyson, before I was married to you I was married to someone else. I am so sorry to keep this from you. It was a part of my past that I had buried long before I met you."

"By the look on your face, it looks like there is something else."

"Yes. He is here. He is living here. He had found me but you are the one I want to be with. Tyson, you are my true love that I want to spend eternity with. I hope you can forgive me. I didn't mean to…"

"Hush, not another word," Tyson said as he placed one finger over Nadia's lips."

"I have nothing to say. I only have something to show."

Tyson stood up and opened his hand towards Nadia asking for hers. She placed her hand in his and he led her out of the door and too his car.

They arrived in Heaven in only a few short moments. As quickly as Tyson could put the car in park, he was out and opening the door for Nadia. He took her hand and gently pulled her out of the car. They stood directly in front of a small park.

Still holding Nadia's hand, Tyson led her into the tall golden trees of the park. As the bark of the trees grew closer together and became more abundant, the color began to change from gold to silver. The leaves were no longer gold, but made of glass.

The two finally came to a clearing. The grass was soft and white as if they were standing on the back of a polar bear. There were no trees in the opening, only a lake. The lake appeared to be made of solid crystal.

Not letting go of Nadia's hand, Tyson walked down to the edge of the lake. They both stood there hand in hand. Simultaneously they both stepped onto the lake and walked to the center. Tyson pulled Nadia close to him and began moving back and forth. Nadia rested her head on Tyson's chest.

"I do not hear any music," Nadia whispered.

"Do not listen with your ears. Listen with your heart," Tyson whispered back before kissing Nadia on the top of her head.

Nadia closed her eyes and took a deep breath. She could hear a faint sound growing louder. She heard a light whisper amplify into a beautiful song. There were no vocals, only sweet instruments.

The two continued to dance to the light and relaxing music. Suddenly, Nadia noticed the crystal lake illuminate like a television being turned on. The program that was playing was her past. She watched the scene when she met Tyson for the first time. The scene then changed to the moment when they had their first date. The scene then changed to her birthday when Tyson attempted to cook her a birthday dinner and proceeded to burn down her kitchen. She then could see when they made love for the first time. That is when he first told her that he loved her. The next scene was their last moments in the airport together. She could then see Tyson as a decorated angel and she standing by his side expecting their third child. They were both older but happy. She could see their enormous house that resided in the golden city of Heaven.

"What a lovely picture that will be," Tyson whispered.

"We will be so happy, Nadia. We can finally enjoy this place as we are to enjoy it. Let's make this a reality. Let go of everything and everyone else. Love me Nadia. Love me for eternity."

Tyson proceeded to kiss Nadia as he lowered himself while pulling her down. She rested on top of him as they exchanged short, passionate kisses.

For a moment, Nadia opened her eyes and caught a glimpse of what the crystal lake was showing. She saw herself and her husband in the past blissfully happy. This time it was Brenden instead of Tyson. She could see herself meeting Brenden for the first time. Then she could see their first date together. The next scene was their romantic trip to Toronto they shared. The final scene was their magical night when he found her.

The sensations were too much for Nadia. She felt as if her heart could burst with too many emotions

from one too many men. She immediately fell off of
Tyson.

"I can't take this anymore. I can't!" Nadia
screamed as she buried her face in the palms of her
hands.

"Its ok, Honey I'm here. All you have to do is
love me."

Tyson had positioned himself over Nadia. He
began kissing her on her neck and forehead as he
brushed her hair from her face. Nadia resisted his
kisses but that only made Tyson increase his
aggression.

"Nadia you must love me! You must."

Nadia attempted to remove herself from under
Tyson but he held her down. In the past, she could
have easily thrown him off but he was stronger. He
looked exactly the same as in the past, but he was
clearly stronger than before. With a giant push of
effort, Nadia was able to slide herself halfway away
from Tyson, but he forced her shoulders down which
caused her head to slam against the hard crystal lake.

Nadia laid there stymied from the blow to her
head. She could see a blurry vision of Tyson over her.
He had ripped the buttons off of her white shirt

exposing her bra. He then began to rip her skirt until he could spread her legs open. He pulled the crotch of her panties to the side as he began to undo his belt.

"We are going to have a wonderful life together Nadia. You will see. We are going to have beautiful little kids and a nice house. We are going to be so happy, Baby."

As Tyson went to lower himself into her, Nadia decided to make her move and placed a knee into him that sent him tumbling all over the lake in pain.
 She quickly picked herself up and began to run. She did not stop for her purse or shoes. His yells for her did not reduce the rate of speed her feet carried her. She ran until she disappeared into the trees until they returned to their golden hue.

Chapter 18

When Nadia made it to the open park area she stopped and had the instinct to hide behind in nearby bushes. As she peered out, she could see angels frantically searching the vicinity. She assumed that Tyson had contacted them to capture her on first site. There was one question that lingered in her head. Why would he request angels and not patrolmen? She did not think that Tyson had the authority to request full fledged angels. Despite not knowing the answers to these inquiries, Nadia knew that she could not allow them to take her into custody. She wasn't sure of the next step but the first step was not to be caught. She moved in secrecy through the shrubbery plotting her escape. She realized the area they were in was slowly being reduced to her area.

She finally saw a way out. Across the park, she could see the top of a passing gondola passing in the golden river. If she timed things perfectly, she could run past her pursuers and jump onto the gondola and float away. She would have to use every bit of stealth her nerves could muster. She eagerly waited in the bushes slowly watching the top of the gondola slowly approaching. She crouched on the balls of her feet waiting to pounce like a snake on a mouse. Finally her anticipation was now ready to be converted into action as the gondola was now in range. She gave quick glances to the left and right and then leapt out of the bushes. Before she could remove her lower torso from the bushes she felt a hand clasp over her mouth and drag her back into the shadows.

"Nadia, please. Don't fight. Don't fight. It's me, Brenden."

Nadia ceased her attempt to escape from his grasp. She looked into his clean shaven face and calm eyes and she knew she was safe.

"Brenden, they are out to get me. If you are caught with me, you may find yourself in big trouble with me. You need to get away from me."

"No they are not after you. It's me who they are after. I have found some horrible information. They don't want this information to get out. It would cause a panic, Nadia. If they catch me they will kill me. I have to give this information to you. You decide what you want to do with it. You can empower people or save yourself. It's up to you. I love you enough to give you this gift. No matter what happens, I will always love you."

Brenden did not have another moment to elaborate on his information or his feelings. The angels began to search the bushes and were lurking closer. The next gondola was quickly approaching. Now was the only time they could escape. Brenden took a firm grip on Nadia's hand and they both made a dash for it.

"Stop," shouted a loud and familiar voice that immediately petrified the two of them.

Nadia and Brenden turned around to find the angels staring directly at them with Tyson in front of them. His eyes were intense and encircled in red. His

face was so intense the veins on his temples bulged
and a large crease formed down the center of his
forehead.

"So this must be husband number one. You
know a few moments ago I was worried that I may lose
her to you but now I feel much better now that things
will turn out alright for me. My Nadia would never
side with a terrorist."

Tyson then turned his attention to Nadia.

"Do you know he is plotting to ruin Paradise?
Did he tell you he wants to ruin the hopes and dreams
of everyone here?"

Nadia looked into Brenden's face. His face
mirrored Tyson's intensity back in his direction. Tears
slowly began to trickle down from his eyes.

"You son of a bitch," Brenden slowly muttered
through is lips which were bleeding from biting it.

"I have been waiting for this moment for a long
time. I wanted to pay you back for a long time."

"Do the both of you know each other?" a
confused Nadia asked.

"No I don't know any terrorist," Tyson
answered.

"Oh you remember me you bastard. Think back! Think back to the night at the hospital. You remember when you murdered me in cold blood."

Nadia was stunned. She was stunned that it was Tyson who took Brenden away from her. It was the man she loved and honored for so long that caused her so much pain. She never realized she was living with a cold murderer.

"You are the one who is a murderer!" Tyson shouted. It wasn't a hospital that you were at it was an abortion clinic! You are the murder! I am a liberator! I liberated a child like I am liberating my wife now."

Nadia stood in the midst of the shouting. She could no longer hear the words that were exchanged between the two men because her thoughts were too loud. She thought of how she was stuck there with the two men that she loved with all of her heart. She wondered how such a thing could happen in Paradise. She had many questions about the events that she had witnessed since she arrived.

She thought of the situation Milner was in with his business. He was living his dream but the cost of living that dream outweighed the reward.

She thought of Rodney and his goal of being the first to graduate college from his family. He always wanted to do something positive to make his family proud rather than bring shame to it. He was accomplishing that goal but he suffered for it. He worked long hours for little money and little time for school.

There was Beth who suffered for so long not knowing her parents and being torn away from the woman she loved. Even when she was with her love, it was shrouded in secrecy.

She thought of Tyson. He was now involved in a structured system that he fought so hard against on Earth. He could not even see the he had been consumed by a military organization. He was forced to watch the only love of his life stand next to another man.

Her thoughts then focused on Brenden. He also had to endure the fact that his wife had moved on after he spent years waiting for her. Not only did she move on, but she married the man who had murdered him. He also never got to see his only child.

Her thoughts then focused inward. She knew only pain since arriving. She spent so much time looking for Tyson, living a nightmare each night of being away from him. When she finally did find her husband, it was her original husband whom she had suffered the agony of loss. She found her daughter only to lose her. Work was more of a burden than joy. The worst of everything was it was up to her to make a decision between Tyson and Brenden. It was up to her on how this story would end. It was a decision she could not bare to make. She could not bring herself to do it despite knowing that prolonging the decision only inflated its weight. She seemed trapped in a life of pain. She was permanently fixated in a love triangle that was meant to last forever. She wondered how this could be Paradise when everyone that was there suffered.

        Her eyes widened. Her mouth opened to its maximum diameter. It was if everything around her had stopped. Her mind had computed an answer to all of her questions that she could not handle. She had come to a realization that was so shocking she would have committed suicide at that moment if it were possible. She looked at Brenden who was still yelling vehemently at Tyson. He did not need to tell her his secret because she now knew what it was.

The only thing that came to her mind was to run. She immediately began to run down the sidewalk. Shouts from the men did not reach her ears. She ran so fast she could not feel her feet hitting the golden sidewalks. She did not bother to see if she had knocked anyone over in her haste.

She ran until she reached the Main Building. It was the building where she had picked up Brenden. It was also the building that was restricted from everyone. She saw the angels guarding the front door. They ordered her to stop yet she continued to run toward them and the door. They went to draw their swords but before they could unsheathe them, Nadia removed two pencils from her pocket and formed a cross with them. The angels went sprawling in terror and out of her way. She opened the large doors to the main entrance and ran inside.

Nadia ran through the main hall that had a ceiling that seemed twenty stories high. The inside seemed too large to be housed in the structure in which she entered. The inside did not have the golden shine as everything from the outside but a darkened reddish hue. As she ran toward the end of the hall that was hidden in shadows she could feel intense heat coming from that section. The heat was so intense it stopped her where she stood.

She then saw the origin of the heat that warmed her clothing and skin. She saw two large glowing red lights that were large enough to dwarf school buses. Two large red horns appeared emerged from the darkness. The size of the horns alone sent fear running through the insides of Nadia. Each one could have been ten stories long. Nadia heard a loud rumble coming from the section that sent her running for her life in the other direction. As she ran past the long glass windows she could see where the red hue was coming from. The beautiful golden sky was a bright red. The marshmallow clouds were replaced by steam. The bright suns that illuminated the sky were bloated fireballs that scorched dead trees in the desolate parks. The beautiful buildings were old broken ruins. The streets that were made of golden liquid were slow moving rivers of thick blood. The handsome angels that glided through the sky were flying corpses that had wings of a mosquito rather than large white feathered wings. She could see the children from Dundon staring at her through the window. They were not children, but men and women in their fifties. Their eyes were large and completely filled with black. The world that she thought was so perfect was actually a barren place full of despair. She was looking at the true reality of this place. It confirmed what Brendan wanted to tell Nadia.

The instant Nadia ran out of the front door, she was grabbed by Brenden and tossed over the side of the stairs just in time to avoid the gunfire from the angels. Holding hands they both leaped off of the sidewalk and into the golden water. They swam downward until Brenden saw an opening that resembled a sewer system on Earth. They both swam through the opening and away from their followers.

They swam into darkness not sure of their destination. They then saw a light ahead of them. They swam toward the opening to find themselves caught in a current. They swam as hard as they could to the bank of the river they were in. They had arrived at a cornfield. They were out of Heaven because everything was its intended color. They made their way to the muddy banks and stared at the endless maze of maize.

"Rurlaw," Nadia thought to herself.

Instincts told them both to enter the maze of corn. They quickly yet silently moved through the rows. They could hear the shuffles of angels searching for them. They could hear the blade of their swords chopping down stalks of corn in search of them. They could see slight glimpses of the soldiers intensely looking for them. If any drew too close, they would vanish into a collection of closely planted stalks. They both turned left from one row to another only to find themselves face to face with Tyson.

"If you want to live, follow me," he said.

"Why should we trust you?" Brenden questioned.

"So we can settle this later and keep my wife alive."

The three of them quickly moved in and out of the rows of corn avoiding the sword toting angels. They methodically moved their way closer and closer toward the house that belonged to Frank and Joanne. When they came to a clearing they spotted a collection of angels. Brenden and Nadia quickly leaped back into the stalks of corn as Tyson stepped out.

"Sir, they are not in the cornfield. Shall we check the house?"

"No. They are in that cornfield!" Tyson shouted.

"I know that my area is secure. I want you men back in there and stay in there until you have found them. I want those two found!"

"Yes sir," the soldiers said in compliance as they went back into the cornfield.

Brenden and Nadia quickly leaped out of the cornfield and the three ran up to the house and let themselves in. They found Frank and Joanne sitting in the living room watching Television and sipping lemonade.

"Well hello Nadia. How are you? Have a seat and Joanne will get you some lemonade."

"We can't stay. We need to use your car," Nadia told them.

"Well where on Earth are you going?"

"There are things happening that I cannot tell you. In time you will know. Please."

"Well we have to go to the market and do some shopping and pick some flowers and…"

"I am an officer of the law. We are taking possession of your car in the name of our Lord."

"They keys are on the table," Frank said quietly.

Brenden quickly grabbed the keys. As the group headed out of the front door, Joanne took hold of Nadia's arm.

"Honey, whatever you do be careful."

Nadia did not say anything. She just stared into the old woman's glossy eyes.

"We have to go now," Tyson said as loud as he could without shouting.

"Goodbye, Dear."

The three of them climbed into the truck that seemed to be from 1957 and drove down the dirt path.

By nightfall they had reached Tundron. This was apparent by the snowfall that lazily fell from the sky. Tyson parked the truck on the side of the road and the three of them climbed out and began to walk through the forest at a fast pace.

"Hurry this way," Tyson encouraged.

"There is a place just up this way where you can be safe for now."

The three of them walked quickly at an incline until they reached a thick collection of trees.

"Just through that way, there you will find peace and quiet."

"This does not erase what you have done, but thank you," Brenden said.

"Don't flatter yourself. I didn't do this for you. I did this for Nadia. I'm keeping Nadia safe. I don't want to make a Martyr of you. She will see for herself where she belongs and I will then gladly send you to the other side."

Brenden gave Tyson one last glance as he took Nadia's hand and began to walk through the collection of trees. Nadia looked back at Tyson wondering if she was truly leaving with the right man.

"Don't worry, we will be together soon enough," Tyson said to her.

"Be safe with him for now."

Nadia and Brenden cleared the thick trees and walked a short way. They did not see any building or shelter but they continued to walk a short way. They walked until they could walk no more. They had come to a cliff that looked over a deep drop into an icy river.

"There is nothing here. He could have at least left us the car if that was the case. Damn him," Brenden said angrily.

"I'm going to go back to the car and maybe rip out the seats or get some material to make a tent or something."

Nadia and Brenden turned around to find three angels standing in their way. There were trapped between them and the cliff. Standing triumphantly in front of the angels was Tyson with a blank stare on his face.

"Did you really think that I would just hand you my wife?"

"You bastard she is my wife. She has always been my wife! She was never truly your wife!" Brendan yelled violently.

"I was the last man she married. She is mine."

"Tyson, you are working for evil. Can't you see that?" Nadia pleaded.

"Evil? No I don't think so. On the contrary, I am working for good. I am working for a purpose."

"You are working for Satan!"

"Satan? Last time I checked Satan lived in Hell, Nadia," Tyson said laughing.

"What do you think this place is?"

Tyson face began to intensify and his voice grew deeper.

"Does this feel like Hell? Everyone is fed in Hell? There is no homelessness in Hell?"

"Tyson, feel with your heart. You know this place isn't right. Everyone has suffered here."

"You're wrong Nadia. I have not suffered. I have flourished! I have become the man you wanted me to be. I am not perfect thanks to our Lord whom you call Satan. I will have you. Life will be perfect."

"How can you just devote your life to evil?" Brenden asked.

"You are the one to talk about evil you baby killer! The Bible told you Satan is evil? A book of propaganda is what The Bible is! A story told by one side. We have all seen which side is the good side. We have seen what ways the other side resorts to in order to get ahead! If you have seen what I have seen, you will know that this is the good side and which is the evil side!"

"Tyson, please…"

"No Nadia. There is no negotiation! I love you with all of my heart. Please come with me. You are starting to sound brainwashed. Don't let him take my wife away from me. Don't let this baby killer kill you too!"

"Tyson I can't serve Satan. I just can't! Brenden wasn't the one who was killing babies. He was there because I sent him there. He convinced me to keep the baby but after you murdered him I decided to abort the baby!"

Tyson lowered his head as he rested his hands on his hips. He then slowly looked up with tears streaming down his cheeks.

"Then you are no longer my wife. He has killed you like you killed your baby."

"I won't let you kill my wife!" Brendan shouted.

"She was my wife. Your vows were till' death do you part. When you died she was no longer yours."

"Well that means that your vows are null and void," Peter said walking from out of the trees.

He stood in front of Brenden and Nadia.

"Peter, get out of the way. I don't want you to get yourself hurt. There are people that need to be processed."

"I am not going anywhere," Peter said as he slowly raised his hands to protect Brenden and Nadia.

With one motion of Tyson's finger two angels quickly approached Peter. The first angel went to throw a right punch at Peter but he caught his wrist and snapped it as if it were a twig. The angel yelled in horror before Peter punched his chin upward snapping his neck. Peter then unsheathed the angel's sword while spinning and slicing the next angel from his abdomen to his neck spraying blood all over the white snow. In a downward motion, Peter threw the sword which lodged into the throat of the third angel sending him squirming to the ground.

A stunned Tyson attempted to surprise Peter only to have his fist caught by Peter. Peter then kicked down at Tyson's right shin causing his femur to stick out of his leg. Peter then punched Tyson in the face causing him to fall to the ground screaming in pain.

Peter then grabbed Nadia and Brenden by the collar and began to fly away with them.

Nadia peeked back at the cliff and saw a bloody Tyson stagger to his feet. Blood from the snow and his face covered his clothing and the tips of his hair. He slowly took a bow off of his back. He then reached for a single golden arrow.

"Hurry and grab onto my arms," Peter shouted.

Tyson prepared his bow and took aim at the three of them. As they both hurried to get to Peter's arms, Tyson let his arrow fly. As it came closer it seemed to pick up speed. Nadia yelled just before she felt the heat from the explosion.

Chapter 19

Nadia gained consciousness staring at a clear blue sky. She could see silhouettes of birds streaking across the bright sun. Tall long leaves surrounded her. Slowly she gathered her senses and slowly sat up. She immediately looked down at her legs. She was relieved to see that they were still intact. When the explosion hit the last thing she could remember was feeling fire grasping for her legs. It was apparent to her that they held onto Peter's arms as he moved them to another location just in time. There were a few questions that she asked herself.

"Where am I?"

"Where is Peter?"

"Where is Brenden?"

"Did they also survive?"

She gingerly stood and took one step. She did not see that the leaves were wet and she went tumbling down a slight hill. Once again she stood, but this time took careful steps in the wet grass.

Nadia walked for ten minutes. She was completely surrounded by extremely tall trees topped with long leaves that resembled floppy ears of a happy dog. Among the trees she would spot vibrant colored birds and a variety of small insects. She would run into a snake and a few monkey-like creatures from time to time but neither the wildlife nor she paid any attention to one another.

Eventually Nadia made it to a clearing. There she spotted a lagoon that was filled with clear water that had a greenish tint from the reflection of the surrounding trees. At the far end of the lagoon, there was a large waterfall that gently lowered fresh water down to the surface. On the left side she could see a body lying flat and motionless.

"Brenden."

Nadia grabbed a large leaf lying on the grass and rushed over to the lagoon. She scooped a small amount of water and trapped it within the leaf. She rushed over to Brenden and doused him with the water.

"Hey are you trying to drown me?" Brenden yelled.

"Brenden you're alive."

"Alive? Yes. Dry? No," Brenden said with a laugh.

Nadia immediately jumped on him and began kissing him passionately.

"Now you're trying to suffocate me."

They both stood up and began to look around. They noticed a small stream leading away from the lagoon. They followed the stream into the forest. It led them out of the forest and to an open grass that rested next to a vast ocean. They both immediately became frightened when they saw someone at the edge of the ocean.

"Don't be startled. Please come down," Peter said.

Brenden and Nadia made their way to Peter where he was bent over washing his hands and glasses in the water.

"I'm glad to see you're both alright," he said as he stood and turned toward the couple.

"Thank you so much Peter. You have been such a help to me since I have come here," a tearful Nadia said.

"Oh there is no need to thank me. That is what my job is right?"

Peter placed the glasses on his face.

"Nadia, when I gave you a tour I told you there were six suburbs of Heaven but I showed you only five. You asked me about this but I did not answer. It is because this area is forbidden by the government. I have never been able to understand why it is forbidden. I am assuming it is too close to the other side. This area is not controlled by either side. Not even the angels have been here. I sneak here from time to time to find solitude. Here you will find plenty of food to last you. You will have to build your own shelter and make your own clothing but the materials are all here. You both should live happily amongst yourselves here."

"Peter, won't you be staying here with us?" Brenden asked.

"No. I must go back. If I stay here they will find all of us for sure. Besides, it is something I must do."

"No Peter you can't," Nadia cried

"Peter, they will certainly do harmful things to you," Brenden added.

"What will they do? Send me to the other side?" Peter said with a laugh.

"Whatever they do to me I am happy with everything that has transpired. I always had questions about things and now I know the answer. I was alive but I was not living. I have finally lived. My life is now complete. Thank you, Nadia. Thank you for showing me life."

Peter took time to wipe away his tears. Nadia went over to him and hugged him.

"I didn't think love was for everyone but you showed me different. I still have not felt love from a woman, but I have seen with you and Brenden. Thank you. Thank you for giving me the love of friendship."

Peter pulled a tearful Nadia away and went over to Brenden.

"Take care of her. Make sure she doesn't fall off of a cliff or anything," Peter said laughing.

"Thanks Peter," Brenden said quietly.

Peter turned around and slowly began walking toward the trees. Before he entered he turned around and gave a smile and a wave.

With one step, Peter vanished into the trees.

Brenden and Nadia were now left alone in their secluded suburb. Hand in hand, they slowly walked along the edge of the water.

"Well here we are," Brenden said.

"I hope we will be safe here," Nadia said.

"No matter what, we are together."

Slowly the clouds began to swirl and grow darker. The breeze grew colder and picked up speed. The tall trees began to bow to the east. The sky was completely black and thunder could be heard in the background.

"We have been found," Nadia yelled.

Brenden clutched her hand.

"Whatever happens we are going to do it together."

The both of them stood in the grass waiting what was to happen next. Brenden looked at Nadia and gave her one last long kiss.

Brenden was then struck on the head by a falling envelope. He bent down to pick it up and was stuck by another.

"Where did these come from?"

Three more envelopes fell from the sky. They both ran toward the tall trees for cover. As soon as they were covered, a downpour of envelopes fell from the sky. It was literally raining letters. After ten minutes the storm subsided and the sky was now clear and the sun was out once more. The breeze slowly began to blow all of the letters away. Each letter was addressed to someone. Nadia and Brenden emerged from the trees to the warm sun. A single letter floated down from the clear sky and Nadia caught it. It was addressed to her. She quickly ripped away the envelope and began to read the letter aloud.

"Nadia,

I hope this letter reaches you. I have doubts that it will because I had never received any letters when I was there.

I am thinking that if you do get this letter more than likely you realize that you are in Hell. I pray that you are safe and doing the best you can to get by.

I am great here in the true Heaven. Here there are no suburbs. Everyone lives in the same city. It's not an actual city but a place. More like a garden. Mary and I live in a very large home. There are no police, or pollution or commotion here. All of the people that I thought I would find where you are I have found. I found my grandparents. They told me to tell you that they love you.

Mary was here fighting my case. They found that I was placed in Hell by mistaken identity. The angels from this side came to rescue me. They looked so scary that night because the black protectant that shielded them from the intense heat of Hell. The eye contacts also protect their eyes from burning out. Once you are exposed to the truth for forty eight hours, your mind and body can not be adjusted to the lie. I will fight to have the both of you liberated as well. There will be a war soon. Our army isn't as large as Satan's but I believe our technology is superior and our angels are more righteous. I have a good feeling our side, the good side will prevail.

I am so happy here with Mary and my grandparents. We all love you and look forward to seeing you and Brenden someday. Yes the right choice is Brenden. Tyson is a murderer and his heart is cold. I love you and Dad. I can't wait to see you all up here someday.

Love,

Beth"

Brenden hugged Nadia as they both cried. Brenden kissed Nadia and wiped away their tears.

That night they returned to the lagoon. Brenden built a fire near the water where they roasted bits of coconut at the fire.

"Can you believe that we are in Hell? I am sure that Heaven is far better than this but I am just happy to be here," Brenden said as he moved Nadia next to him.

"It gives a new term to see you in Hell," Brenden said as they both laughed.

"Hell?" Nadia asked mockingly.

"We may burn. They may rip our flesh apart. But we are together. Hell or Heaven, if I am with you there is no place I'd rather be."

www.ingramcontent.com/pod-product-compliance
Lightning Source LLC
Chambersburg PA
CBHW030414020726
47493CB00003B/1062